Bitter Frost

kailin gow

Bitter Frost
Published by THE EDGE
THE EDGE is an imprint of Sparklesoup LLC
Copyright © 2010 Kailin Gow

For information, please contact:

THE EDGE at Sparklesoup
P.O. Box 60834
Irvine, CA 92602
www.sparklesoup.com
First Edition.
Printed in the United States of America.

ISBN: 1-59748-898-4
ISBN: 978-1-59748-898-3

DEDICATION

✳

THANK YOU TEAM AT SPARKLESOUP AND THE EDGE FOR WORKING SO HARD TO MAKE THIS BOOK SERIES COME ALIVE - ESPECIALLY TARA, KATHY, LINDSEY AND JIM. ALSO THANK YOU TO DARLA FOR SUCH A BEAUTIFUL COVER. A LOT OF LOVE HAS GONE INTO THIS BOOK AND ITS CHARACTERS. THANK YOU FOR COMING ALONG WITH ME ON THIS JOURNEY AND MAKING IT A FUN AND HEARTFELT ONE.

Prologue

✴

The dream had come again, like the sun after a storm. It was the same dream that had come many times before, battering down the doors of my mind night after night since I was a child. It was the sort of dreams all girls dream, I suppose – a dream of mysterious worlds and hidden doorways, of leaves that breathe and make music when they are rustled in the wind, and rivers that bubble and froth with secrets. *Dreams*, my mother always told me, *represent part of our unconsciousness – the place where we store the true parts of our soul, away from the rest of the world.* My mother was an artist; she always thought this way. If it was true, then my true soul was a denizen of this strange and fantastical world. I often felt, in waking hours, that

I was in exile, somehow – somehow less myself, less *true*, than I had been in my enchanted slumber. The real world was only a dream, only an echo, and in silent moments throughout the day it would hit me: *I am not at home here.*

I would shake the thought off, of course, dismiss it as stupid, try and apply my mother's armchair psychoanalysis to the situation. But then, before bed, the thought would come to me, trickle through the mire of worries (boys, school, whether or not I'd remembered to charge my IPod before getting into bed, whether or not my banner would be torn down yet again from the homeroom message board) – *will I have the dream tonight?* And then, another thought would come to me alongside it. *Will I be going home again.*

And the night before my sixteenth birthday, the dream came again – stronger and more vivid than it had ever come before, as if the gauzy wisp of a curtain between reality and dream-land had at last been torn open, and I looked upon my fantasy with new eyes.

I was a fairy princess. (When waking, I would chide myself for this fantasy – sixteen-year-old girls should want to start a fruitful career in environmental activism, not twirl around in silk dresses). But I was a fairy princess, and I was a child. I dreamed myself into a palace – with spires reaching up into the sun, so that the rays seemed to pour gold down onto the turrets. The floors were marble; vines bursting with flowers were wrapped around all the colonnades. The halls were covered in mirrors – gold-framed glass after gold-framed glass – and in these hundred kaleidoscopic images I could see my reflection refracted a hundred times.

I was a toddler– perhaps four, maybe five years old, decked out in elaborate jewels, swaddled in lavender silk, yards and yards of the fabric – the color of my eyes. I hated the color of my eyes in real life – their pale color seemed to make me alien and strange – but here, they were beautiful. Here, I was beautiful. Here, I was home.

The music grew louder, and I could hear its melody. It was not like human music – no, not even the most beautiful concertos, most elaborate sonatas. This was the music that humans try to make and fail – the language of the stars as they twinkle, the rhythm of the human heart as it beats, the glimmering harmony of all the planets and all the moons and all the secret melodies of nature. It was a music that haunted me always, whenever I woke up.

Beside me there was a boy – a few years older than I was. I knew his name; somehow my heart had whispered it to my brain. *Kian.* All the palace around me was golden – with peach hues and warm, pulsating life – but Kian was pale, pale like snow. His eyes were icy blue, with just a hint of silver flecked around the irises; his hair was so black that ink itself would drown in it. He seemed out of place in the vernal palace that was my home – out of season with the baskets of ripe fruit that hung down from the ceiling, with the sweet, honey-strong smell of the flowers. But he was beautiful, and all the more beautiful for his strangeness.

We were dancing to the music, our bodies echo-ing the sounds we heard – or perhaps the sounds were echoing us. We were learning the Equinox Dance. It was the dance that we would dance on our wedding day.

It was a custom in this fairy kingdom that royal children would learn this dance – the most com-plicated and mysterious of all dances – for their wedding days. And so we all practiced, day after day (night after dream-rich night), for the day that we would come of age, and dance the dance truly, our feet moving in smooth unison, echoing the commingling of our souls.

My father was the fairy king of the Summer Kingdom – a place where everything tasted like honey and felt like the morning sun on your forehead. Kian's mother was the Winter Queen of the Winter Kingdom, a place beyond the mountains where cool breezes turned into arctic chill, where a castle made of amethyst stood upon a rocky peak, and evergreens dotted the horizon. And it was only fitting that our two kingdoms should meet, should join together; we were the chosen ones.

"You will be my Queen," the boy whispered to me. His voice was confident, strong.

The dance was still difficult for us. I got tangled in my waves of lavender satin, tripping over his silver shoes. He in turn kept fumbling with his hands, trying to spin me around the waist and instead, elbowing me in the side – but somehow it didn't hurt.

"Silly," cried the other girl watching us. She, like Kian, was stunning – her hair was as long and lustrous as a starless night; her eyes were silver, like the pelt of a wolf. She was called Shasta, I knew. "Silly – that's not how you dance." She giggled, and her eyes glittered with her laugh.

And then everything changed and became chaos – my home was suddenly ripped apart and replaced by a new scene. Something – *something* – was attacking, something with teeth and horns and claws that ripped, something that made a great and bellowing sound I could hear even when I pressed my hands tightly to my ears. *The Minotaur.*

The screaming came from all directions; everybody was running – me and Shasta and Kian – and the adults, all of them– away from the Minotaur, into each other. Everyone had gone mad. And then someone – someone – was fighting it, a cavalcade of fairy knights each shining in his golden armor – and some knights from the Winter Kingdom too, in their silver.

The Summer King and Queen were there, and the Winter Queen was there too. She looked like Shasta, but older– and her face was different. There was something hard and glinting in her eyes that I could not see in Shasta's, like the shiny specks in stone. I was afraid.

"This is your fault!" a voice snapped – I could not tell to whom it belonged.

"No – it's yours!" Another voice – equally angry, equally cold.

"If it hadn't been for your kingdom…"

"Don't give me those excuses – the Minotaur is a device of your court!"

The voices grew higher and stranger, angrier, louder, quicker and quicker in their retorts until I felt like I was surrounded in a cacophony of rage, bellowing over and over again until at last all I heard was:

"It's all because of that girl!"

And for a moment, they were all silent, and all of them were staring at me.

I could not understand, but it did not matter. Before I could think, could understand what was going on, what was happening to me, the scene had changed again.

I felt his arms around me. That was the first thing; I felt it before I could see anything, see him. I felt his arms encircle my shoulders, feel him brushing my shoulder blades lightly with his fingertips. I shivered. His hands took mine. I could see him. It was Kian, but he was older, now, and so was I – both a young man and a young woman – staring at each other. Age had only made us more

11

beautiful; his hair was longer, now, and his eyes sharper, with greater depth. I could see my reflection in his eyes; my hair was longer too: a deep, warm brown with flecks of gold studded throughout. And I could see my expression – full of fear, full of joy – as he bent down closer to me, as his lips came ever closer to mine.

"Oh, Breena," he said to me. "My Breena."

His blue eyes took on a look of sharp determination; he stared at me with such intensity that I felt that his eyes had penetrated into the truest part of my true soul, a part hidden even to the rest of this strange and wonderful land.

"I will kill you, Breena. It is what I have to do. It is decreed." He cupped my face with his hands, and I could feel his cool breath whispering upon my cheek. "We are mortal enemies."

Always, every night, that same dream – that same fear, that same joy. When I woke up each morning, I felt a profound sense of loss, a yearning that stretched so deeply it crossed the bounds of reality itself. The alarm clock would ring, and everything would change. I was a nearly-sixteen-year-old girl, with suede boots, with T-shirts bearing sayings I believe in. I had an IPod, a cell phone, my laptop (with pages full of html code for my brain-child, teensforgreatergood.com). I spoke in rushed slang about the latest films and television shows, played video games with Logan, teased him when he won, teased him when he lost. I wore little to no makeup and complained about homework during G-Format. The idea of dating – of fumbling high school boys trying to score in between stolen keg stands, of Facebook relationship statuses and hastily-texted endearments – repulsed me.

But for a few hours each night, I was somebody else. I was a princess in a castle, with a dress made of lavender and besides me there is a prince with arctic-blue eyes, and arms wrapped closely around me, and lips coming nightly ever closer to mine...

I was home.

Chapter 1

✳

It was not the best day for a birthday. The sky was misty and full of rain – clouds looked as full and wet and ready to drip as kitchen sponges. I woke up with a headache, in a feverish sweat. – *The dream again.* A prince in disguise. A melodious dance. The Minotaur, all eyes, all teeth. I tried to shake the images out of my brain.

"Mom!" I called out.

There was no answer.

This was strange. There was a tradition in my family – every morning on my birthday, my mother would surprise me with a birthday breakfast in bed: banana pancakes with cinnamon and chocolate powder swirl. It was her way of trying to put some weight on me.

"Mom?" Maybe she had overslept. I briefly considered bringing her breakfast in bed, to tease her. I crept into her room. It was empty.

"Mom?" My calls ricocheted around the rooms of our house, but there was no answer. I was alone. Her coat and hat were missing from the downstairs rack. She had gone out, then. Had she forgotten my birthday?

I didn't have time to think about it. I was late enough for school as it was, and my birthday did not preclude the school bus arriving in five minutes down the block. I threw on the cleanest clothes I could find – a soft, silky T-shirt and a slightly battered pair of denim jeans – and dashed out of the house towards the bus stop.

I made it, but only barely. I was winded, breathless; I didn't even have the breath to bid my customary hello to the bus driver. The sky looked more miserable than before. This was not my morning, I concluded; I hoped this was not a sign of things to come.

I pressed my head against the frosty glass of the windowpanes, feeling the cool air blow softly on my cheek. The bus sped on, through our little suburban town – a sea of identical, winking houses, of elegant gardens trimmed perfectly in accordance with the Town Council's meticulous landscaping policies. And then we entered the woods.

The long, winding country road that took us through the woods to Kennedy High was my favorite part of the journey to school. The woodlands were deep and green, the sort of endless forests in which one can imagine all kinds of daydream fantasies. These woodlands, currently under development by the Town Council, and marked for transformation into a Gregory County Buy-B-Mart, were my lunchtime sanctuary, the place I spent my stolen free hours wandering when I could not bear school any longer, could not stand the crowding mean girls and the taunts of the popular crowd and the politics of cafeteria seating; I could not bear the idea that these trees – these rich, green trees – might be torn away, replaced with shiny, glinting asphalt and meticulously arranged parking lots.

"Tree-na," they called me. It was a stupid nickname, the sort of thing probably thought up on a drunken binge through Court Spade's parents' liquor cabinet some Friday night when his family was out of town. It was certainly nicer than the names that they called some of the other nerds. But nevertheless, it stung.

Today, however, the woods seemed unfamiliar to me. The old pathways seemed to curve and wind in strange ways as I passed; the trees seemed like they were whispering to me, their branches contorting in angles I did not recognize. The rustle of the leaves was strong – but there was no wind. Something was different.

And then I saw a satyr on the edge of the road.

It vanished a moment later. Fantastic, I thought to myself. My sleeping patterns had led me to hallucination at last. But the image stayed with me – that little figure, with a man's face and torso and the legs and hind of a goat, with little horns poking through right above his ears. It was not unfamiliar to me. I had read the books of Greek and Roman mythology my mother had bought me for my tenth birthday so many times that the pages were dog-eared and falling out; I knew exactly what a satyr was meant to look like. I also knew that they weren't real.

Just a hallucination, I thought, a trick of the brain. Perhaps I had fallen asleep again, dozed back into my enchanted dream.

That was when I saw the goblin, poised atop the school building. It was blue and hunched over, with tiny bat-wings that didn't look like it could carry its bony body. And then it took flight...

Just a bird, I thought to myself. Just a bird, like any other. I'm the one who's strange today – I haven't gotten enough sleep. (I had seen its eyes, its claws, its eerily pointed chin...)

I did my best to ignore the mysterious sights of the woods. I had enough on my plate as it was.

My day did not improve. Some days before I had hung up a "Save the Woodlands" banner on my homeroom's notice board along with a sign-up sheet, hoping to co-opt some of my classmates into an effort to save my beloved woods from the machinations of the town council. Somebody had torn it down, shredding it into little pieces and leaving it scattered on the homeroom floor. Nobody had bothered even to clean it up. Figures, I thought. The popular kids at school were given tacit approval for their actions by the teachers, who in turn wanted to impress their generally wealthy, influential parents.

This is why I liked the woods, best. There was nothing there but me and my thoughts"– no cruelty, no distractions. Only the sound of the whispering stream and the crunch of leaves beneath my feet.

I sighed and began picking up the pieces of my banner.

"Need some help?" Logan came up behind me.

I smiled at him gratefully. "Yeah, sure."

"Happy birthday, Bree."

He'd always been my best friend. He was my age – though much taller (a recent development – I had teased him all through our early adolescence when I towered over him easily). His hair was light, sandy-brown, his eyes hazel with gold specks, and his demeanor warm, even protective. I always felt safer when Logan was around. He smelled like the woods – like wood chips and musk – for, like me, he spent all of his time wandering its hidden pathways. His family were country people – if they didn't live in the woods themselves they lived as near it as possible – not in the whitewashed, sterile houses of the suburban part of Gregory, Oregon.

"Sorry they tore up your sign-up sheet, Bree," he said.

"No worries. We were the only two who signed up. Oh well. Not like anyone at this school cares about anything more significant than who's sleeping with who in celebrity news. They're probably just excited that we get a Claire's Accessories within walking distance of school – probably think an endangered species is something you have to pick up on the sales rack before it sells out..."

"I wish they were an endangered species, considering how mean they were. Whether they believe in the same things are not, they didn't have to tear up your sheet," said Logan, giving me a great bear hug.

My day did not improve. I suffered through another round of P.E. – a subject at which I was notably terrible – before returning to the sweat of the locker room, ready to face the barrage of mean girls who saw, in that strange way only girls can understand, the locker room as a way to show off their toned, sleek bodies, expensive underwear, and even monogrammed towels to their less affluent peers.

Clariss and Hannah, the heads of this unfortunate cabal, had already selected for themselves the choicest seats in the locker room.

"Really, Hannah," Clariss was saying. "I don't know how you're ever going to get a boyfriend if you don't at least go to third..."

"I don't want to be a slut like Elizabeth Macneal," said Hannah.

"Big Mac's only a slut because she's fat," Clariss decided, as if this logic were entirely sound.

I tried to shut out their voices – squeaky, high-pitched sounds.

And then I saw the goblin again. It was smaller, this time, perched on the edge of Clariss and Hannah's bench, snarling at them like an angry dog. It stuck out a sharp talon and started sniffing.

It was real this time. I blinked – and it was still there, opening its mouth and aiming precisely at Hannah's hand...

"Stop it!" I cried, and tried to swat the goblin away. "Go away!"

Before I could collide with it, the goblin vanished, and my hand instead hit Clariss square in the arm. The bottle of perfume she was holding dropped to the floor and shattered, the sticky-sweet smell of expensive scent flooding the locker room, combining with the smell of shampoo.

"What are you doing?" shrieked Clariss. "Are you crazy?"

"Yeah, what the hell, Tree?" Hannah echoed her.

I felt a pair of hands shove me into the lockers. "That was Chanel No. 5, you dumb bitch!"

"Crazy hippie," said Hannah – as usual, her echoes only a few nanoseconds too late to be anything but pathetic imitation.

I was surrounded by them – like a caged animal. Hannah and Clariss were joined by the rest of their coterie – Ali Walsh, Cassia Barraclough, and Jo Murphy, all of whom had decided that I had stepped out of line, and were to be punished.

"Why don't you go draw some *fairies*," Jo said, shaking out her auburn hair.

"No wonder she always draws magical creatures," said Cassi. "She doesn't have any real friends of her own."

"Maybe she can put a spell on someone," Ali said, cackling as if she had achieved the height of wit, "make them be her friends."

They all started laughing, pointing, and joshing each other until at last I could stand it no longer. I pushed past them out into the hallway, my eyes stinging with the first hint of tears.

"Enough," I said to Logan at lunchtime. "I can't wait to graduate. If I get into art school, I'll be out of here – making my fortunes in Providence, Rhode Island." My dream was to go to RISD – the Rhode Island School of Design and become an art director like my mother or a famous artist with my own art gallery.

"Only a few more years," said Logan. "Then you're free."

"Being a sophomore sucks," I decided.

"Yeah," he said. "Not as bad as being a junior, though. College applications."

"Don't remind me," I said. Logan was smart. He was already a junior although he was just a few months older than me. I had no doubt he would be accepted into any college he set his sights on.

We caught sight of Clariss, Hannah, and the gang staring at us, passing around their whispers and their giggles.

"What do you think they're saying?" Logan asked me.

"The usual. Probably how hot you are, and wondering why you spend all your time with weirdoes like me instead of dating one of them."

"Don't be stupid," said Logan. "They're probably talking about how *gorgeous* you are! It seems to me they're just jealous of you." He moved in closer as a student carrying a large tray nearly sideswept us. Our hands brushed. He glanced over at me for a second and said, "Bree, you're perfect."

"Hah, that'd be the day," I said. "Besides, what's this I hear about you asking Clariss?"

"What?" Logan made a face. "Who told you that?"

"I overheard Hannah telling Ali Walsh, Clariss was going with you. Somehow I figured I'd better do my fact-checking before jumping to conclusions."

"Check away," said Logan. "The closest I've come to asking Clariss to the prom was when I was standing in front of her, listening to her talking about how much she wanted to go, but just couldn't find the *right guy to go with... so* I told her I wished her good luck, and walked away."

"Why didn't you go with her?" I was trying to sound nonchalant, but there was a bit of envy trickling into my voice. Clariss was, after all, the most beautiful girl in school. And Logan was the most gorgeous boy in school, although he was my best friend since whenever.

"Because she didn't ask me," said Logan. "I like a girl who isn't afraid to be herself, and ask me if she wants to go with me, instead of playing games." He saw my face. "Beside she's not my type."

"What is your type?"

"Natural, down-to-earth," he said, looking at me with a hint of a smile.

Before I could respond, I hear a familiar lilt behind me. "Guys guys guys guys guys!" exclaimed Sandy, a tiny redhead with what seemed like a constellation of freckles dotting her nose. "Oh my God, guys!"

"Yes, Sandy?"

"They found Jared!"

"Jared Dushev?" Logan stood up, looking concerned. Jared had been missing for about a week. We all assumed he'd been cutting class to go up to Portland for a Depeche Mode concert – it was the sort of thing Jared would do.

"He was in the woods! Apparently they found him near the Love Shack, completely out of his mind – babbling so that nobody can understand him, covered in human bites!"

"Oh my God – is he okay?"

"Apparently he's lost a lot of blood. We don't know yet."

"Is it drugs?" I asked.

"Maybe. Jared's into that sort of thing. But the bites..." Sandy shivered. "I don't like the woods; they're creepy. Ever since the wolf attack."

She dashed off, eager to check another name off her list of people to whom to gossip.

"Things are sure strange around here," I said to Logan. "First Jared – now, you know – I think I'm going crazy. Whatever I saw in the locker room... human bites... next thing I'll find out this whole town is haunted, like in – *Buffy the Vampire Slayer.*"

I tried to laugh off my worry, but Logan remained silent, his brow furrowed. He stared at me with quiet intensity, his dark brown eyes growing larger as they stared into mine. For a moment, I thought he looked frightening – as frightening as the morning's woods – even predatory.

"What is it?" I asked him.

"Nothing." He smiled at last, and I could have sworn his teeth looked a hint sharper than was normal.

I rubbed my head with my hands. I must be seeing things again, I thought. Time to get some sleep.

Chapter 2

✳

But there was no sleep to be had for me. Instead, there was Algebra Class, followed at last by Art – the last class of the day, and a respite from the chaos and confusion the day had brought with it so far. Art was always my favorite class – I took such pleasure in losing myself on the canvas. There, I could bring out all the images I had seen in the most secret part of my soul, paint the moments and people and figures from my dreams, express myself more deeply and truly than I had ever been able to in any other medium. My paintings were filled with fairies and demons, pixies and goblins, satyrs. Even today, of all days, seemed somehow better, easier to deal with when I was painting. I painted the satyr that I thought I had seen – the goblin poised to take flight from the rooftop. Even

28

if I was going crazy, I thought, at least it was improving my art. Plenty of artists were crazy, after all. Van Gogh had even cut off his own ear. I grimaced at the thought.

After Algebra I met up with Logan again.

"I've been thinking," I said. "I think something's going on today – something big."

"Like your birthday," he teased me. I smiled.

"I mean – these things I've been seeing. First a satyr, then that goblin. Something's different about today. And I think we should find out what it all means."

"Your point being?"

"Research, Logan."

"You want to research mythical beings? You're not going to find that in any library," Logan laughed.

"Actually," I said. "I am. The library has a whole section of Greek myths, Egyptian myth, even English and Norse. Just because we're not going to find Pixie information in a natural history textbook doesn't mean they're not there somewhere."

"Myths aren't real," said Logan. He did not meet my eyes.

"Actually," I said, acutely aware that I was putting on my nerd-voice (Logan rolled his eyes with a

29

smile), "myths reflect centuries of oral tradition in non-literate as well as literate peoples – when it comes to the supernatural, there's no beating folklore."

"You sound like your mother," Logan said with a grin. When it came to slightly pedantic discussions of myth, legend, and folklore, my mother could go on for hours. It was the reason my family had few friends in Gregory.

So to the library we went, in search of information about the sort of creatures I had seen. There was little mention in the first book we tried, *Bulfinch's Mythology*, nor was there much help in any of the works about Norse mythology. We were ready to give up before I found relevant passages in Edward Causabon's *The Great Book of Anglo-Saxon Folk and Legend: A Mythological Dictionary*.

"Wait, wait here," I said. "Here's something."

Goblins. The book read. *Mythical beings believed to have trickster powers – they are commonly cited as maintaining human form, albeit with minor exceptions (longer claws, pointed chins), and often used in mythology as a stand-in to represent minor demons. While goblins were widely understood as mischievous creatures, and somewhat malignant, they are rarely depicted as actively seeking to harm humans in the manner of, for example, the Pixie. For more, see PIXIES.*

"Hey, take a look at this," I said. "Pixies..."

Pixies. One of the most malevolent figures in English mythology, Pixies is understood as the counterparts of faeries. While the magic of the faeries is often cited as dangerous, even fatal for non-humans, faeries themselves are rarely understood as being evil or malicious in and of themselves; rather, they are depicted as belonging to an entirely separate world than that of human beings. Rather, Pixies – traditionally the enemies of either werewolves or vampires, depending on the source – are known for their malicious attacks on human beings, including but not limiting to severe bite marks that leave their victims with intense memory loss and a "touch of madness." Pixies are depicted in a number of Old and Middle English sources, include "The Wyrd of the Wild," "Skanner's Tale," *and several folk compendia from the early thirteenth century...*

"Whoa," said Logan.

"Severe bite marks that leave their victims with intense memory loss and a "touch of madness," I repeated. "Sound familiar to you?" Then I stopped myself. "Wait," I said. "This is stupid. Really stupid."

"You don't believe in *Pixie*s, then?" asked Logan.

"Of course not!" I said. "I'm not... I'm not Treena, okay? The stupid hippie who draws magical creatures out of Disney movies."

"I didn't say that," Logan said softly.

"It's just..." I sighed. "It's just those dreams I've been having. Every night. About fairyland – Feyland, they call it. And it's the most beautiful dream, every single night. And it feels so *real*. And if there are goblins, or satyrs, or pixies in the dream, well, they *feel* real, too. Look, I know it's stupid."

"I don't think it's stupid at all," said Logan.

"Maybe in another life," I said. I groaned. "I should get home," I said. "I have so much homework to finish."

"Not doing anything special for your birthday?"

"I don't know," I said. "My mother and I usually spend it at Baba Louie's – they've got the best ice cream in town. But she wasn't at home today when I got up, and she hasn't called me or texted me since."

"Your mother texts?" he snorted.

"She likes to keep "modern," I said. "But I haven't been able to reach her. Great," I sighed. "Stood up by my own mother on my birthday. How pathetic is that?"

"Not very," he said. "I'm sure she'll be in touch. She probably had to rush to work or something."

"Yeah, maybe," I said.

"Let me tell you what," said Logan. "Sweet sixteen is too special to celebrate alone. Let me come by and cook you some dinner. My childhood as a latchkey kid taught me some valuable cooking skills. And if your mom shows up, just text me and I'll cancel."

I smiled. "Thanks, Logan; that's really sweet."

"No problem," he said. "I like to cook. Especially for someone who can appreciate my culinary skills. And you, my dear, eat like a horse."

My voracious appetite was indeed the subject of many jokes on the part of my friends and family. ("Where does it all go?" my mother threw up her hands in despair).

Feeling slightly better, I caught the late bus home – along with the kids who had stayed late for detention. I curled up against the window, glad that at least I had one friend with whom to celebrate the day. But I couldn't relax. Thoughts kept cropping up in my mind, images – the goblin, satyrs, – *Pixies*....

We passed by the Love Shack, the dilapidated old shack at the end of the woods that was, until the wolf attack on Francesca Kaminski six months ago, the most popular destination for young people to arrange beer-soaked trysts. I thought of Jared Dushev – babbling incoherently, covered in human bites... had a *Pixie* done this to him? Did *Pixies* even exist?

And then I saw it, standing by the side of the road.

I thought he was a hitchhiker at first, one of the backpackers that frequently hiked through Gregory on their way to Oregon. But then I got a closer look at him.

He was tall – too tall, somehow, for his slender frame, so that he seemed to dangle down from his narrow, bony face. His cheekbones were high and pointy, triangulating down into a sharp, cruel chin. His hair was ashen blonde, and his eyes were green – a weird, neon color I had never seen before, too bright and strange to be natural. His hands – with long, snakish fingers, rested upon a sharp staff.

Delano. The name came to me before I even had time to realize what I was seeing – and I recognized him, even as I had no idea who he was.

The bus rolled on towards him.

And then he turned to me. It seemed that the bus had stopped, or at least slowed – time itself was pouring out like molasses. I could see the nebulous color of his eyes twist and shift – first it had been green, now it morphed into yellow. He could see me. Through the foggy glass panel, through the bus, through the distance, he could see right into me. My heart started ricocheting around my ribcage.

Breena.

I heard a voice call my name, in a sound so high-pitched, so unearthly, that it could not have been human. The figure was ten yards off at least; I felt his call as a whisper in my ear.

When I got off the bus I ran home, locking all the doors and windows behind me. I was out of breath, terrified. I tried to calm myself down – *Pixies* didn't exist, after all – Jared probably was experiencing the bad after-effects of an unfortunate drug trip. But *how did he get those bite marks?* The world of my dream seemed to be hovering parallel to reality, the tender fabric between the two fluttering aside – my dreams trickling into the world of day.

"Hello!" I called out. Still nobody at home.

I dialed my mother's office.

"Raine Malloy's office?" the voice answered. It was my mother's secretary, Paula.

"Hi, Paula; it's Bree. Do you know where my mother is?" She should have been home by now.

"Oh, Bree, hi. Look, I'm really sorry, but your mother had to be called out of town on some really important business. I had to call her at six in the morning – she didn't want to wake you. Told me to tell you how sorry she is, and to wish you a very happy birthday. She'll be back soon. It was an emergency, trust me."

"Oh," I said. "Sure." At least she had remembered. All the same, this didn't sound like her. Something was wrong.

Worry knotted itself into my stomach.

Suddenly I heard a loud rapping at the door. I jumped, thinking of the figure – the – *Pixie* – I had seen on the bus ride home. The *Pixie* that had seen me.

The knocking came again. I couldn't breathe; panic seeped into me. *Delano.* The terror was instinctual, irrational – as if my soul understood somehow what my brain could not.

The sound came again. Then the fumbling of the door knob. I crept backwards, looking for something I can use as a weapon.

Then I heard the voice.

"Hey, Bree? Bree? Are you there? I've brought ice cream!"

Relief flooded my veins. Logan. Of course.

"Just a second!" I smoothed my hair, shaking all the worry out of me. How could I have been so stupid as to forget?

"It's freezing out here!" Logan called. "Everything OK?"

I went to answer the door.

Chapter 3

✳

"I brought groceries," said Logan, with a smile. "Your favorite tortilla bread, some chicken..." Before he could finish his sentence, however, I dragged him inside and locked the door.

"What are you so paranoid about?" he asked me.

"Nothing," I said sharply. "It's stupid. Nothing."

"It doesn't sound like nothing."

"You'll think I'm stupid," I said. I turned red. The rational, sensible, modern-day part of me could not believe that I was going into hysterics about perceived *Pixies* or theoretical fairies. Sixteen-year-old girls go into hysterics about math grades and prom dates, I thought (although that didn't seem like too enticing a prospect either), rather than hallucinate *Pixies* on the roadside.

"I don't think you're stupid," Logan said, taking my hands in his. "The only stupid thing is you getting upset and not talking to me about it."

"I think..." I sighed. "It's crazy, okay. But I think I saw the *Pixie*. On the road home – standing as the bus went by. I think he saw me."

Logan jerked up. "What did he look like?"

"Pointy face – white skin, – *really* white skin – and his eyes."

"What about his eyes?" He leaped to his feet.

"Green, kind of. But yellow – sort of – you know glow-sticks that change color when you break them? Sort of like..."

"Stay right here." Logan began marching, one by one, to the windows, checking that they were locked, closing the curtains. "Don't move – don't answer the door, no matter what."

I had expected him to tell me to stop worrying, that Pixies and fairies and magical creatures were only figments of my imagination. If anything, I had expected him at his most open-minded to cock his head and consider the possibility of supernatural fauna. I had not expected this.

He came to me and held me closely, so closely I could smell that reassuring, familiar smell of musk and wood lingering on his neck. He pressed his lips to my forehead. "Feel safer?" he asked me. He had calmed down now, and felt more like the Logan I knew. *My* Logan.

Of course, I thought to myself. He was just making me feel safe – making sure I knew he was protecting me. There was nothing to worry about at all.

"Come on, let me make you some dinner," said Logan. "Enough with the stress for one day." He smiled. "I've got lots of options for you. Mexican tortillas with fajita chicken, Italian pasta with meatballs, or Chinese noodles with shrimp. I think we should eat them all. But save room for dessert" – I've got a surprise for you."

"You're amazing."

"I'm average." Logan shrugged. "Besides, it's your birthday. If I'd brought my guitar, I could have even sung you a song. And," he added, "I believe you mentioned you'd finished your latest painting?"

"You remembered!"

"I don't suppose you're going to let me go without seeing it."

I blushed. "It's not that good…"

"I'm sure it's excellent," said Logan. "Come on – show it to me."

I brought the canvas down from the art studio upstairs. "See," I said. "Mediocrity at its finest." I was embarrassed, showing my pictures to Logan. His confidence in me, his faith and his trust, had the effect of making me want to live up to his expectations, no matter what. He thought I was a great artist – I wanted my paintings to be as great as he thought they were. I hoped whatever Logan saw in me was really there.

"Bree Malloy," said Logan, examining the canvas. "You are a genius." It was a painting from the dream. They were always paintings from my dreams. Whenever I woke up from a particularly vivid evening in Feyland, whenever the lilting music of the fairy waltz had played too long and loud in my ears, I woke up with a desire, a craving to paint. The unreleased energy would haunt me all day – through school, through lunch, through the afternoons – until at last I would be unable to bear it a moment longer and would dash to my studio, feverishly painting from memory the images in my brain – the bared teeth of a Minotaur, the turrets and spires and minarets of the golden Summer Palace, the face, preternaturally beautiful, of a fairy prince with winter eyes....

This one was of Kian. I had painted it a few nights ago – when the dreams had started getting stronger. He was a young man in this painting, strong and powerful, with cheekbones that glimmered like ivory and eyes fringed by dark lashes, that seemed to shine out of the painting, shine with a light that no oil on canvas could ever have rendered naturally. He was standing in a garden, ripe with orange-flowers and yellow blossoms, the tropical colors of the garden contrasting sharply with his cool, unblinking stare.

"It's so realistic," Logan added. I noticed that he was looking at the background – the landscape in which I had painted Kian – almost willing himself to ignore the details of the prince's face.

"What's wrong?" I asked him.

"Nothing," he turned red.

"Is the portrait all right?"

He nodded, refusing to look at me. "Is that the guy from your dream?"

"The *man*," I said, defensive in spite of myself. "Yes, from my dream" My face fell. "You don't like it?"

"No, it isn't that," Logan said. "He's beautiful. Beautiful. It's just" – the detail... you've an eye for details, Bree." His voice sounded forced. "They're really – they're really lovingly done." He sighed. "Come on, Bree, let's get some food. I vote that we start with a certain favorite delicacy of yours. Three guesses."

"What is it?"

"What wakes you up in the morning, cools you off in the summer, and can only be found in your favorite chain coffee store?"

"A caramel latte?!" I leaped up. I had not had one since May; Gregory didn't have one store (although the proposed woodland shopping mall, to my intense frustration, was due to get one), and my commitment to environmentally friendly behavior meant that I didn't want to waste the gas to drive all the way to neighboring Vanton.

"I bought ice cream, coffee, and this weird syrupy-stuff from the corner shop." He poked the canister suspiciously.

"Let's try it," I said, eager to let the subject of the paintings drop.

It was not quite chain-store quality – it was messy, and our efforts rather stained the countertop I had just finished cleaning – but it was delicious. "Whipped cream on top!" I proclaimed, grabbing a canister from the pantry and foaming the top of the cup with a pyramid of whipped cream. I missed the cup slightly, accidentally aiming at Logan and getting whipped cream all over his shirt.

"Nice going!" said Logan.

"Oh, God, Logan," I breathed, "I'm so sorry. That's your favorite shirt!"

"Well, you should be," he snapped, grabbing the canister from me. "You know why? Because now! Now! Now your shirt's going to get ruined too!" His mock-anger gave way to gleeful joy as he aimed the canister square at my face and started squeezing.

"Gotcha!"

"Not so fast!" And so we began chasing each other around the living room with the whipped cream canisters, laughing as we did so. The worries of the day were forgotten – at last we were relaxed, carefree, and normal. Pixies and fairies and Jared Dushev seemed far away as we joked and teased each other. We were kids – normal kids – having a food fight in a living room while my parents were out.

At last we gave up (Logan having won a rather sound victory), and I went upstairs to change. "I can just wash my hair out in the sink," I said, putting my head under the cool, refreshing water. Logan, meanwhile, had taken off his shirt to let it dry.

"I bet Clariss just wishes you sat around shirtless in her house," I said – and I cannot deny that I certainly allowed my glance to linger on his lean, taut muscles a few moments longer than would have been strictly friendly. Despite being in Oregon, Logan had a natural tan as though he spent a lot of time outdoors without a shirt. Not only had he grown taller in the last couple of years, but his frame had filled out – broad shoulders and chest down to a taut tapered stomach. Logan had a body any athlete would envy.

"Yeah, well, I'd sure like to empty a canister of whipped cream in her face," said Logan. "Maybe then she'd shut up."

"You really don't like her? Not even a little bit?"

"Yeah, that's why I'm not going to prom with her. Because I'm desperately in love with her."

"No, seriously, Logan."

"Firstly, she's horrible to you, and I don't care if she looks like Keira Knightley, that's a deal-breaker. Secondly, she's really not that attractive. All that makeup, hair extensions, and straightener – I don't even know what she looks like under all that stuff. If she isn't confident enough to look like herself..."

"You're like the perfect boy," I said to Logan, coming over from my impromptu shower, my hair dripping all over the floorboards.

"Not quite," said Logan, and his smile darkened. For a moment, he looked unhappy.

"Hey you, come here."

I grabbed a clean kitchen towel, wrapped it around my head, and sat beside him.

He took the towel and started rubbing my hair dry. "You've still got some whipped cream – right there." He gestured to a stray bit still clinging to the hairs beside my face. "Let me get it for you." His hand stopped at my cheek, cupping it softly. I looked into his eyes"– they were full of intensity, full of kindness.

"I've had a great birthday," I said, softly.

"It's a pretty good day for me, too," he said. His hand was still there. "Happy birthday, Bree..." His face came closer, ever more slowly, to mine.

My heart began beating more quickly. "Yeah, you too," I said instinctively, before realizing what I had just said. "I mean..."

"Yeah..." His other hand found mine. I felt myself leaning forward, just slightly, my lips just inches from his...

Suddenly there came a loud knock on the door.

Something was wrong.

It was a booming, vicious knock – the kind of knock that echoed through the house and seemed to make it shake.

"Breeana!" came a voice from outside. "Breeana!" It was high-pitched, unearthly, terrifying. It was the Pixie's voice. *Delano.*

Logan sprang up. "Go upstairs," he said, roughly.

"Logan, what's going...."

"Don't argue with me – go!" He knew something. I could see it in his eyes, in the tautness of his muscles, in the fierce setting of his mouth.

"Hide in the art studio. Lock the door, get on the floor, and *don't. Move.* Whatever you hear – whatever you *think* you hear – Don't. Move."

There was no time to argue. I ran.

Chapter 4

✳

I could not breathe. I could hear the knocking get louder and louder downstairs, hear Logan rushing down, but I could not wrap my head around what was happening. "Logan!" I tried to cry out but my voice refused to listen to me, to make any sound at all; I choked. What was he doing? Whatever was down there – whatever *thing* – and I knew deep in my heart that it was the Pixie, Delano, the thing I had seen staring at me on the side of the road – it was surely nothing Logan could fight. He was just a boy, after all – strong, surely, muscular, certainly – but a human. Like me. He could not fight against some magical creature.

And yet – what magical creature was there? Until this morning, I hadn't believed in magic at all; now, it was coming all too quickly.

He had been so strong, so sure, Logan, I thought. He had taken control of the situation – he had believed everything I said, taken it seriously, then rushed me upstairs and had me lock myself in the art studio. *Why?* It was almost as if he had known what was going on, recognized the situation from what I was telling him, and determined that he would fight the Pixie.

What did he know?

The door flew open; I could hear the sound of a whistling wind swoop into the living room. It was the sound of a thunderstorm. My heart was beating faster now; terrified, I scrambled under the desk, covering my head with my hands. There was a loud *crash*.

What was going on? Who was this thing – this Pixie? And what did it want with me?

My eyes caught sight of the painting I had done of Kian, sitting back on the easel where I had replaced it, and my heart felt that same familiar longing – that same familiar familiarity. I felt as if there were something I had forgotten, some grave and important fact just slipping beyond the grasp of my brain, some key to all the answers of my dreams, of this whole strange day, that I knew – that I had always known – but just could not remember.

And Kian's face was the key to it all.

I closed my eyes tightly, my mind straying back to the world of my dreams.

Come on... I whispered to myself. *Come on, Breena, remember...*

Remember whatever it was I had forgotten.

There came a great and terrifying howl from downstairs, the howl of a wolf, careening off the ceilings and the walls, echoing upwards so that it felt the howl was coming from directly behind me, from all around me. The floors of the art studio shook; the walls were vibrating. I could hear one set of plates crashing, then a vase – identify each sound as one thing, then the other, crashed, was destroyed. I could hear sounds of a struggle – great *thumps* followed by loud *crashes*, the sibilant hissing of the wind on all sides of me, seeping underneath the door, shaking at the lock.

Make it stop... I cried. *Just make it stop...*

And then at last it had stopped, and the silence that followed was worse than the fight itself.

One way or another, it had finished, and I did not dare to get up, to go downstairs, to see one of them (oh, but which one?) lying dead upon the floorboards, and one of them standing before me.

It didn't matter, I told myself, willing myself to be brave. If Logan had won, and sent the Pixie away, then he would need my help – washing the wounds, getting bandages... If Delano had won, then he would be coming upstairs to find me shortly... and the end result would be the same. I had to be brave.

You are a princess, said a voice in my head. *Be brave.*

Somewhere, somewhere far away, deeper than every plummet sound, I heard the melody of fairyland, that strange waltz from my dreams. It was playing for me. It was willing me to be brave.

Slowly, I opened the door.

I came downstairs, feeling sicker and sicker at each step. I did not want to see what had happened.

The first thing that caught my eye was Logan. He was laying naked, unconscious, thrown upon the sofa. But he was breathing.

I grabbed a blanket and ran to him, covering him up, without even the presence of mind to be embarrassed. He was hurt, and that was all that matter. I knew enough First Aid Training not to move him, nevertheless I shook him a bit, calling his name.

"It's going to be okay, Logan." I pressed my cheek to his heart. It was beating strongly, powerfully. He would be fine. "Listen to me" – there's just a little wound, okay? Nothing too bad." I grabbed the shirt he had taken off earlier, pressing it to the cut on his shoulder, applying pressure to stop the bleeding. "You'll be fine."

There was no sign of the Pixie. I relaxed, taking the first full breath I had taken since that terrible knocking first rapped on the door.

I went to the window, checking the locks, making sure there was nothing lurking in the woods.

And then the kitchen door flew open.

He was taller than I had remembered; his face was bonier, his eyes even more yellow – the putrescent color of burning sulphur. But I remembered his smile from the bus well enough – that cruel, cold, evil smile that told me he could look upon me, and Logan, in full, clear knowledge of what exactly he planned to do to us, and feel no regret, no remorse, no hesitation.

"*Breena.*" His mouth had not moved, but I heard his voice bearing down upon me, freezing the blood in my veins. "*Come here, Breena.*"

His eyes remained fixed upon me.

And then he was changing. He was beautiful, almost – and charming – his chin became less pointy – his eyes turned green again. Why, what had I been so afraid of, I felt myself wondering. He wasn't so bad at all. He was even handsome, with his outstretched hand, his long, ash-white hair. (And somewhere in the back of my mind a voice kept on screaming, kept on resisting, but I kept on moving forward anyway, hypnotized, entranced by his beauty, by those mesmerizing, morphing eyes...)

Perhaps I could just go to him, just for a little while...

Something stopped me. I felt a hand – a warm, strong hand – clamp around my mouth, another arm encircle my waist.

"Logan?" I craned my neck, but Logan was still there, lying unconscious upon the sofa where I had left him, still breathing.

Then who was behind me?

I struggled, but the grip remained firm on my waist, pulling me backwards, away from the Pixie

King, whose malicious eyes (for they were back to malicious, now) were still fixed upon me.

I whipped my head around and gasped.

I knew his face, knew his face better than I knew my own reflection. I had dreamed of it every night for sixteen years.

It was Kian.

He was more beautiful than I remembered – that I ever could have known. His hair was longer, now, and his skin was even more white – the color of the first snowy morning in wintertime. His eyes were the silvery-blue of a wolf pelt – I could have mixed a thousand colors together, but I would never have been able to paint his eyes as I saw them then, in all their evanescent beauty.

And he was pulling me away.

"Wait," I said, pushing myself out of his grasp. "Wait"– look – we can't leave Logan here."

But he kept on pulling me, floating backwards, up the stairs, towards the art studio.

Prince or no prince, I wasn't about to leave Logan in the clutches of the Pixie King. "Let me go!" I cried, trying to loosen his vice grip upon me. I remembered the Kian from my dreams – soft and gentle, even loving. This wasn't right.

"Let go of me!" I cried, but it had no effect. We were nearly at the studio now.

Then I caught sight of the Pixie King. He wasn't any more keen on Kian taking me away than I was, and he had fitted his bow with a sleek, silver arrow, and was aiming it right at us.

In a choice between the two of them, I still would have gone with Kian.

"No!" I cried, but it was too late. He had already drawn his bow, his sinewy arms tensed up, ready to fire the arrow straight into my heart...

Suddenly, out of nowhere, a blur leaped upon the Pixie, knocking him to the ground. It was some kind of animal, I thought, but it was certainly bigger than any animal I had ever seen. Its fur was long and gray; it had endless claws, and huge teeth. It was like a wolf – but it wasn't a wolf. It was different, somehow – nobler – the way unicorns in *Causabon's Mythography* looked different from ordinary. The wolf had been touched by magic.

The Pixie King leaped up again, ready to strike at the wolf, which in turn bared its teeth and snarled viciously. The two hurled themselves at each other, locked in battle, ready to fight to the kill...

And then Kian starting pulling me back again, into the art studio, away from the wolf, away from the Pixie, inextricably bound in the struggle of death...

He swept us backwards and the art studio door closed before us.

And then the door vanished.

I looked around us. We were in a forest – a great expanse of glittering trees, shimmering leaves. This was no ordinary forest.

"Where are we?" I asked Kian, but somehow I already knew.

I had been there before. My skin was tingling. My heart was pounding. I felt as if I had, for the first time in my life, woken up from the haze of sleep. Everything was clearer, brighter, sharper, more colorful. I could hear music in the wind – echoes from miles away. I could see each leaf, each blade of grass, each chip of bark, with infinite clarity, as if I were looking under a microscope.

I had painted some echo of this place. But if all my paintings were imitations of the images in my brain, then the images in my brain had always been only echoes of this.

We were in Feyland at last.

Chapter 5

I looked around me. It was the most beautiful forest I had ever seen. The leaves sparkled, each one giving off a glow like so many tiny fireflies. The grass murmured beneath me, rolling like waves over the earth. Everything was alive, moving. I could smell lavender and honeysuckle in the air. And everything had a sound, a song. The leaves had their song, and I could hear it – the gleeful, light bursts of a pitch pipe. The bark had a song, and I could hear that too – deep, powerful bass notes. The wind had a song – the trills of a piano sonata – and I could hear too the song of the clouds, slow and melismatic. And the songs came together, too, into a great symphony of sound, and somehow the sound had *color*, too, because I could *hear the col-*

ors, and I could *see the smells*. Somehow my senses had been scrambled, overwhelmed by the beauty of the forest. My dreams were nothing like this. Nothing, not even the most unbridled flights of my imagination, could ever have compared to his.

And then I realized how I had gotten here; I remembered Kian, forcing me up the stairway, forcing me to leave Logan, with his hand clasped over my mouth and his ears deaf to my struggles.

Beautiful fairy prince or no fairy prince, I wasn't about to let anybody carry me anywhere.

And so I bit him.

It was the first thing I thought to do – the first bit of flesh I could grab – so I sunk my teeth into his hand and began kicking wildly. He jerked his hand out my teeth and glared at me– I saw where my teeth had left a gleaming, silver stain upon the whiteness of his palm – and tried to restrain me. I closed my eyes, trying desperately to remember the self-defense tricks I had learned in my mother's Female Empowerment classes. – *Knee to the groin. Fingers to the eyes.* My limbs shot everywhere, trying to find his weakness, some way to hurt him, to get away...

My mother's tricks, however, had been designed for human attackers. Kian gracefully dodged every blow I tried to land at him, vanishing and reappearing behind me, parrying me with the slightest feint to the left, a block to the right. At last I rushed straight towards him, my heart banging against my chest, my cheeks flushed with rage.

"Oh no you don't," I cried.

He caught my wrists and twisted my arms around, until I was facing away from him. I could feel his breath upon my neck as he whispered in my ear.

"Are you going to stop struggling?" he asked me.

"Not until you tell me what's going on!" I cried, feeling almost out-of-breath.

But it was no use. He held me fast and firm.

I had dreamed of this moment often, dreamed of his hands on me, his lips so perilously close to my neck. Even at that moment, I could not deny that part of my weakness was psychic – an innate submission from the deepest cloisters of my subconscious. But I wasn't prepared to let my instinct take over. Nobody, not even Prince Kian of Feyland himself, was going to kidnap me and get away with it.

"Fine," I said at last. "Now, tell me what you want and let me go. And apologize."

"For what?"

"For grabbing me like that."

"Princes don't apologize," said Kian. I turned to look at him, flushing with anger. I had thought he was merely being arrogant, but he seemed genuinely confused. Then his expression changed. "You don't have to worry about your friend. I know that must have frightened you. But the Pixie won't drink his blood. Pixies don't like werewolf blood."

"Werewolf blood?" I sputtered. "But Logan's not..." I recalled his eyes when I had told him of the Pixie, his strange response to my intimations of supernatural occurrences. He had believed me, hadn't he – hadn't he taken everything more seriously than I had myself? I was too tired to resist. It didn't seem that much stranger than anything else that had happened today.

"But of course, you already knew that, didn't you?"

"Of course not!" But before the words were out of my mouth I knew that perhaps I was lying to myself. That connection I had always felt with Logan – the way he smelled of the forest, the way I felt so comfortable showing him my paintings of Feyland. Perhaps I had always sensed that he, like me, was touched by magic. I smiled grimly. On a far less philosophical note, there had to be some explanation for him choosing to hang out with a loner like me over Clariss and her ilk.

I had, however, far more pressing issues to consider, not least among them the safeguarding of my own life.

"Are you going to drink my blood?"

I thought of Clariss, who squealed with sensual glee at the thought of attractive young vampires, and often sighed over films depicting bloodsucking fiends in romantic entanglements of girls of my age. She was welcome to Kian, I thought. I certainly wasn't interested in being murdered before I turned seventeen.

He considered. "You'd be a delicious treat for plenty of species in Feyland," he said. "The Pixies would have you for breakfast. I'm afraid, however, that I'm far more keen on Fairyfruit wine than on the blood of the innocent, if I haven't offended you."

Was he teasing me? There was no sign of a smile in his eyes.

"Only animals like Pixies drink blood. Fairies are far too civilized for that."

"So – you're almost human!"

He looked somewhat offended. "I think you'd better say that humans are almost fairy."

"I'm afraid I wouldn't know." I stiffened. I wasn't in any immediate physical danger, but I wasn't particularly interested in being overly polite to the man who had just kidnapped me.

"Surely you haven't forgotten what it was like at the Courts?"

I thought of my dream. "No, I've never been here before," I said. I certainly wasn't prepared to give away any more information than was strictly necessary.

I could tell he didn't believe me. "Really, now?" he said. "Haven't you ever dreamed – say – once or twice, of a place you couldn't describe? Of a place you couldn't quite put your finger on – but that was more familiar to you than your own home, your own bed?"

I couldn't lie to him; he could see right through me. "Yes," I said at last. "As long as I can remember I've been having dreams. But that was all it was. A dream. I don't know why I'm here."

"Was it a dream?" Kian began pacing down the length of the forest. I saw the grass respond to his approach, and part – making a path in the dense underbrush. I gaped.

"Maybe you thought it was a dream," Kian continued, breaking the spell of my distraction. "But you were here – living here – once. In your childhood. And then in your dreams – coming back to visit. You and I played in the Summer Court, with my sister Shasta. We hid oranges and bid each other find them. We splashed in the fountains and tried to chase phoenixes – we never caught any; phoenixes are wily birds. We even learned the dance for our wedding."

"*Our* wedding? I was a child!" (And yet I could not help feeling somehow that I had always known this. I had painted him – over and over again. It almost made sense… I forced the thoughts out of my head. Delano the Pixie had almost hypnotized me into attraction to him. Why should I be so sure Kian wasn't doing the same?)

"Our parents arranged it," Kian shrugged.

I thought of my mother arranging my wedding and laughed. She was a firm believer that women should remain unmarried – and unhindered – as long as possible, and explore as many different avenues of romance in the meantime.

"I doubt my mother would have gone in for that," I said.

"Oh yes," Kian said. "Yes, your mother Raine, and your father the Summer King."

I put the issue of my mother's philosophies on marriage aside for a moment. "The Summer King?" I burst out laughing. "That's ridiculous! I don't even know what a Summer King is?"

"More or less what it sounds like," said Kian, with a somewhat exasperated expression. "The Summer Court is ruled by a Summer King."

"Well, yes, I got that much... so I'm a... a real princess?" I tried shoving Kian playfully, forgetting myself. "Get out. That's the most ridiculous..."

"And I am Kian – the Winter Prince – the son of the Winter Queen."

I stopped him. "That makes no sense," I said. "Winter and Summer are seasons. How can you rule a season? Wouldn't that mean that your family and my family take it in turns?"

He shook his head. "Not in Feyland. In your world, seasons are times. In my world they are places. One where it is always summer. One where it is always winter."

I had questions about how exactly Feyland existed relative to the earth, and how this fit in at all with my basic understanding of physics, but somehow I felt this really wasn't the time.

"And the Summer King is a fairy." Kian continued.

"So I'm a fairy."

"Don't be stupid," said Kian. "You're a half-breed." There was a faint note of contempt in his voice.

"A half-fairy, then," I said, my voice rising. "And I don't see what's so wrong with that."

"The fairy part is rather more pressing," he said. "If you were just a human I wouldn't have had to go through all that trouble to get you."

"What, am I late for our wedding?"

"We're not engaged," said Kian, shortly.

"But I thought you said..." I wasn't quite sure why I was protesting. Surely I should be relieved... instead, I felt vaguely insulted.

"That was before the War of the Seasons," Kian said. "We have broken off diplomatic relations with the Summer Court. Our marriage contract has been rendered invalid."

He took my hand. For a moment I thought he was being kind. Then his grip tightened.

"So I'm afraid you are now my prisoner."

Chapter 6

I couldn't help but laugh. "Your prisoner?" I said. "That's ridiculous."

And then I saw his face. It could have been made of stone, I thought – unblinking, unsmiling intensity. He meant what he said.

I considered my options. I could run, I thought, but Kian was faster than I was – and even if I were able to escape, I had no idea how to get back to my own world. I imagined, somehow, that no matter how far I ran, in any direction, no road in this strange wood would bring me back to Gregory, Oregon. I thought of Logan, locked in vulpine battle with the Pixie King, and shuddered. All I wanted was to return to him, to bandage his wounds, make sure he was all right – but running wasn't going to get me anywhere. I could reason with Kian, I thought, convince him to let me go – but his expression was impenetrable, as icy as his kingdom. A Winter Prince, I figured, wasn't exactly the sort from whom to expect a warm heart.

That left me with one option. Gathering as much information as I could from him before even considering escape. If my father was a Summer King, I reasoned, surely he would have some influence – even if the two kingdoms were at war.

"Okay," I said. "Fine. I'm you're prisoner. You win." I threw up my arms. "But I don't see what good it will do. I live in the human world – not the Summer Court. I'm not even part of this war."

"It was not my decision," said Kian, gravely.

This was heartening. If he wasn't gunning for me out of desire to kill me or keep me prisoner, I might have a chance at changing his mind.

"My mother has ordered your capture," he said.

This was far less positive.

"The Winter Queen has decreed that whosoever should capture the daughter of the Summer King would win great favor in her kingdom."

"So, you got to me first," I said. "But what do you need her favor for? You're her son. Aren't you going to inherit the kingdom?"

Kian smiled, bitterly. "You have evidently not met my mother," he said. "Her favor isn't quite so easy to attain."

"But I am, apparently," I said. "First that Pixie – now you! Seems like everybody's coming to find me. Was that Pixie acting on your mother's orders, too?" Being captured was bad enough, but the idea that several people would be fighting over the bounty involved was even more distasteful.

Kian shook his head. "Pixies have their own agendas," he said, with evident disgust.

"So how did you both find me? It's not like my living room is on the map of Feyland, I assume," I hastily added. Anything was possible. "How do you get from one to the other, anyway?" This was the sort of information I needed. I watched him carefully.

"You gave out a signal," he said. "Unintentionally, I'd wager. You've been hidden well, in that barbarian land, especially in a small town like yours where we have no interest in visiting. But you're of age now."

"Of age for what?" I decided to conveniently ignore the "barbarian nation." There was plenty of time for defending my species later.

"Marriage. Once a fairy is of age to marry, her magic is much keener – other fairies can sense it. With a royal fairy, such as yourself, the signal is even stronger..."

"That's disgusting!" I said. "I'm... in *fairy heat?*"

"I wouldn't put it quite like that," said Kian. "That sort of talk doesn't quite befit a royal maiden. Only a fairy's intended is supposed to feel the signal. The Pixie – they have ways – he might have picked up on the signal."

"And you're my intended."

"Formally," he said.

"But the contract has been broken," I said. "Surely you shouldn't feel any... signals."

Kian smiled. "As a society," he said, "Fairies are obliged to follow much the same rules as humans – laws, contracts, reigns, rules. We cannot simply work on magic alone, anymore than humans can govern their society entirely on violence and power. If we only listened to magical laws, Feyland would be little more than a dictatorship of the strong. So, it is necessary that we have, like you – treaties, contracts, pieces of paper that tell us what we can and cannot do. For a smooth society."

"One that can't even keep the peace," I mumbled.

"But magic – it's still there," said Kian. "And no matter what our laws and contracts say, the laws of magic are stronger. That's why they're so dangerous. I'm afraid that a magical bond cannot be broken quite as easily as a marriage contract."

"Well, my mother says that marriage is a tool of the patriarchy," I said. Clearly, she had some experience with fairy legality. So, Kian was still drawn to me. This could be useful. I decided to conveniently ignore that the feeling was mutual.

"So, magically, I'm still your intended," I said. "You're still attracted to me."

He nodded, saying nothing.

"Then why take me prisoner?" I had no experience of flirting. I imagined it involved batting my eyelashes and imitating Clariss's behavior around Logan. "Surely you don't want to take the woman you love prisoner..."

He rose sharply. "I never said I loved you. There are political concerns at stake, concerns far more pressing than emotions."

"I thought you said that the laws of magic were more powerful than the laws of state."

"I don't deny that," Kian said stiffly. "But that's precisely why the laws of state are required to put limits on the laws of magic. Or else there would be chaos. And right now, Breena, my concerns are for my kingdom. Even a Halfling like you can understand that."

I bristled. "Halfling!" I said.

I heard a light, soft chuckling behind me. I whirled around to see another fairy sitting in one of the trees. Like Kian, he was pale, with dark copper hair that gleamed with a metallic sheen. Winter, I guessed. If I wanted to survive this, it was a good idea to start distinguishing between Winter and Summer fairies straight-off.

"Taking your time, are you, Kian?" said the fairy.

Kian's grip tightened around my wrist. "I've got her, Flynn" he said. "And I'm going to bring her to the Queen myself."

"She's as beautiful as the stories," said Flynn.

"Thank you," I said stiffly, staring him straight in the eyes. I remembered my mother's female-empowerment classes. "If you're a woman alone with men in any situation," she had always told me, "from the workplace to school, the last thing you want is them commenting on your looks. They won't take you seriously."

Then again, my mother had apparently slept with a fairy king. Perhaps her advice wasn't entirely sound.

"Do you intend to run away with her?" asked Flynn. "Or will you hand her over to the Fairy Queen straightaway."

Before I could allow myself to fully grasp what "run away" might mean, Kian shook his head. "I follow the Queen's" – *my mother's* – commands. I, *and nobody else*, will bring her in."

Flynn understood and bowed. His eyes had the look of a hungry wolf, just barely restrained from leaping upon its prey.

"As you wish, my Prince," said Flynn. "But don't delay, or I'll have to bring her in myself. I have been angling for a promotion, after all," he said, fingering the hilt of his sword.

I wasn't enormously keen on Kian, but he seemed like the safest option at the moment. I took his hand. "I'm his intended," I said. "I'll be sure to follow orders."

Flynn saluted Kian and flew off, his wings beating against the sky.

I considered Kian. "You don't have wings," I said.

"Beneath my cloak," he said. "It's considered rather rude to show them in public unless one is mid-air."

"So, I'm a prisoner," I said. "Why don't you contact the Summer Court and get me a ransom? And then I can go home, and you can have some gold – or silver – or whatever it is you fairies use for currency, and we'll forget any of this has ever happened."

"Not so simple," said Kian. "The exchange must be made."

"What exchange?"

"You are a prisoner of war," said Kian. "As is my sister Shasta."

I remembered the giggling girl who had danced with us in my dream.

"In the Summer Court?" I asked.

He nodded.

"Well, I'm a princess, aren't I?" I said. "Let me go and I'll have her released. It sounds fair to me."

"Not so simple," he said again. "The Summer Queen treats her victims without mercy."

"That's ridiculous!" I said. "I know my mother – she's absolutely the nicest woman in the world – a bit odd, but she's certainly not about to start torturing prisoners."

Kian looked perplexed. "The Summer Queen is not your mother, Breena," he said.

"So the King is *married*?"

This complicated things.

"Yes," said Kian.

"No. No!" My mother may have been somewhat – "liberal" – in her views on romance (certainly the population of Gregory, Oregon, had thought so), but she would never have gotten involved with a married man, fairy or no fairy.

"Then I'm not the heir to the throne, am I?" I said. "Surely the Summer King must have some legitimate children."

"No, Breena. The Queen is barren. And the King needed to continue his bloodline..."

"With a mortal? That doesn't make sense."

"It would have been worse, perhaps, if it was a fairy," said Kian. "At least your mother was not a political threat to the Queen. If a fairy had been the mother of a future heir to the throne, the po-litical implications would have been far worse..."

"I take it the Queen doesn't like me very much," I said. If my husband had fathered a child with another woman, I certainly wouldn't be welcoming her with open arms.

"You are correct," said Kian.

"Fantastic," I said. "So I'm the heiress to a kingdom that's ruled by somebody that hates me, I'm your prisoner, I'm being chased by Pixies – is there anyone in Feyland that likes me?"

I was even less popular in Feyland than I was in high school.

"It's a good thing I found you," said Kian. "Plenty of denizens of Feyland want to kill you."

"But you'll keep me alive," I said, relieved. "For Shasta." As far as bad situations were, this certainly could have been far worse.

Of course, given my luck, that was precisely when things got worse. Suddenly, from the edge of the clearing, we heard a series of howls – strange, unearthly howls that sounded like the cross between the roars of a lion and the cackling of a jackal.

Kian sprang up. – "Minotaurs." he said. "Run!"

But they were too quick, all of them – so quick that I could not even make out their shape – only the horns on their head, the bared teeth, the claws...

Kian charged them, his lance and sword in hand, battling one after the other.

I backed up against a tree, making sure none of the minotaurs could get at me from behind. Kian was before me – the sole force between the minotaurs at me.

They scratched at him, covering his arms and face with silver streaks of what must have been fairy blood. One pushed past him as he fought off another, coming straight at me.

I tried to run, but it was too late. The minotaur reared up over me. I caught a glimpse of its eyes. They were black and endless. I could see my death reflected there.

Suddenly I was covered in blood. I heard the minotaur howl, felt its pungent breath on me as it fell backwards. Kian pulled out his sword from the creature's back.

"There," he said.

"Now let's get out of here. I won't have the strength for many more battles without some medicine. And there will be more."

He grabbed my hand and dragged me after him. I resolved that once I had caught my breath, I would demand some form of weapon for self-defense.

Chapter 7

�֍

We tore through the woods, Kian and I. He dragged me along by the hand, running at fairy speed, while I coughed and choked and spluttered behind him. I was just a human, I thought to myself, trying to catch my breath as we jumped over brooks and streams, darted through forest glens and glades, how could I be expected to run as quickly? I didn't even have wings.

"Why can't we just fly?" I coughed.

"Pixies scan the skies – come on!"

I was reminded of my agonizing PE classes at school, where Clariss would constantly outstrip me, her lithe, tan body running rings around my thin frame on the track course. As much as I despised her, I think I rather preferred her to minotaurs.

As we ran, however, I began to regain my breath and my strength. Fairy air had a strange effect on me – or perhaps it was just the fairy blood after all – and my lungs at last seemed to increase in size to take in more air; my legs pushed more quickly at the ground, and soon I was not just catching up with Kian, but nearly leading the way, pushing us through stony cliffsides and along sandy shores. I had little time to take in my surroundings; at the same time, I could not help but be affected by them. The land of Feyland didn't seem to have a discernible ecology – instead, rushing waves and sunny beaches gave way in the space of moments to snowy mountainsides and harsh, jutting cliffs. There were some patches of ground that felt like the tropics – fetid heat, the buzzing murmur of the jungle – and other areas that were like the forest I had first seen. Out of the corner of my eye I glimpsed all manner of creatures – not only other fairies, but mermaids darting in and out of the waves of the sea, centaurs galloping alongside us, the sounds of satyrs' dances in the distance. I had always read my Causabon's – *Mythology* assiduously, memorizing every fact about every magical creature, but I had always thought that these creatures were fictional –

products of the unconscious fears and stirrings and longings of human history. But they were real – the most beautiful and most terrible things that human minds had ever come up with – as real and true as I was. I was one of them.

"Now you've got your second wind," cried Kian, as at last we came to a snowy mountainside, jutting straight out of miles of grass. "You can slow down now; we're almost there."

"Why slow down now? Which way am I running?"

"Just up the path."

"We came at last to a little house made of rock, half-hidden in the cliffside, covered in snow.

"This isn't the Winter Court, is it?" I said, with some not inconsiderable measure of disdain, as we entered. I had, after all, some growing measure of pride for the Summer Court.

"No," said Kian. "I only come here to hunt."

I didn't ask what it was he liked hunting.

"Lock the door behind you," said Kian. I thought of Logan, saying those same words earlier that afternoon (had it been that afternoon?) and my heart grew heavy again.

"So, minotaurs," I said at last.

"Minotaurs," he said. "They, like much of Feyland, are out for the bounty on your head. Either that, or they just want to eat you. Fairies don't speak the minotaur language; we consider them animals."

The conservationist in me leaped up. "Well, just because you don't understand them doesn't mean they're just beasts!"

"Would you have preferred that we stay and chat?"

He did have a point.

I looked around the lodge. It was unlike the Courts I had seen in my dreams – grand, filled with ineffable beauty, awe-inspiring. No, this place was smaller – even – dared I think it? – human. The walls were covered with frescoes – paintings directly on the stone. I began looking at one – a study of a fairy dance. As I stared, the figures seemed to be getting closer and closer to me, as if I were being drawn into their world. Suddenly, they began dancing – first in the painting, and then around me; as I looked around it seemed that I had been transported into the world of the painting, so that I was standing in the midst of the fairy court, listening again to the fairy waltz. I had been to the

Musee d'Orangerie in Paris when I was a little girl, and sat in the "Monet Room" – where Monet had painted on a circular canvas going all the way around the room, enveloping the audience in the story of the painting. It didn't even compare to this.

Kian laughed, and suddenly the images around me vanished.

"You're not used to fairy art," he said. "We paint in three dimensions here. That one is one of my best works."

"You did that?" My eyes widened. "Incredible!" I looked at Kian with a bit of admiration. He was a bit of an artist like I was.

"I'm very proud of it," Kian said.

Before I could answer, there came a knock at the door. We both stiffened.

"No," Kian said presently. "It's safe; open it."

In strode the funniest-looking creature I had ever seen – half-man, half-goat, with horns on his head that looked like they were in perennial danger of falling of.

"Pan!" said Kian. "Good of you to join us. Pan is a satyr, Bree."

"I gathered," I said, a bit more defensively than necessary.

"Hello, beautiful!" The satyr scurried over to me, taking an intrusive sniff of my person. "Well done, Kian!"

"Pan," Kian said, with a warning note in his voice.

"That's fine," I said. "Well done indeed, Kian."

The satyr laughed. "You've got a lot of spunk, missy."

"Bree," I said. I grew a bit more daring. "Princess Bree, if you wouldn't mind."

The satyr's eyes widened. "Of the Summer Court!" He nearly fell backwards over himself bowing. "Sorry, I didn't mean to intrude upon ah, erm, uh, a political affair."

"I didn't realize you had so many young fairy women over, Kian," I said. Of course it was to be expected. He was attractive, after all, and I imagined the fairy world wasn't quite so different from the human world in that regard.

"Pan exaggerates," Kian said, stiffly. "We had an unfortunate run-in with a minotaur, Pan."

"Ouch," said Pan, wiggling his horns. "Ferocious creatures, aren't they, minotaurs?"

"Yes indeed." I turned to Kian. "It would be a good idea for me to have a weapon to fight them off with, don't you think?"

Kian scoffed. "I don't think giving my prisoner a weapon is a particularly good idea," he said.

Pan shrugged. "He's got a point, you know. So," he turned to Kian. "You taking her to the Winter Court?"

"As soon as I've recovered from my wounds, yes," he said. "That is, if the Princess doesn't try to escape again."

"You needn't keep me prisoner," I said, exasperated. "I'm not stupid. If I am royalty, and if you want to trade me for your sister, you're not about to kill me – which is more than I can say about everyone else around here. Give me a weapon; don't give me a weapon. I'm not going to try to run away, so you can stop treating me like a prisoner and start treating me like – well – a guest!"

"How can I know you won't run away?" said Kian.

I rolled my eyes. "Do I look like I want to get eaten by a minotaur? Or bitten by a pixie."

He had to concede that I had a point.

"If you want me to go somewhere, just ask." The whole thing seemed abundantly silly to me. Pixies and minotaurs I could understand. Political treaties and wars just seemed arbitrary. Then again, my mother had been a fervent anti-war protester. Then again, I remembered, my mother had also carried on an affair with a Summer King. I felt vaguely nauseous.

"Very well, Your Highness." Kian's voice was laced with sarcasm. "Would you *mind* staying the night, before we set out upon the morrow for the Winter Court?"

"Why, yes, your Highness," I said. "Thank you kindly for your ever-so-polite invitation. I would be delighted to join you for a marvelous jaunt to the Winter Court! I've been longing for you to ask for ever so long."

Pan laughed heartily. "That's a firecracker you have there," said Pan. "Now, anyone for some fairyfruit wine?"

Fairyfruit wine, I discovered, was designed for fairies – fairly enough. For Kian, it seemed to have a pleasant, relaxing taste; he could drink glass after glass without getting more than merry. For me, I realized, it had a stronger effect – as a half-fairy, I imagined, my tolerance was lessened. I stopped after a glass or two, and resisted Pan's attempts at pouring more into the golden goblet Kian had supplied me for that purpose. Pan, by contrast, clearly had no tolerance for fairyfruit wine; this didn't stop him from pouring goblet after goblet down his throat, washing it down with healthy shots of what he called birch beer brandy. In the end, I think, it was neither the quality nor the quantity, but the mixture, and Pan was astoundingly, uninhibitedly, drunk.

"Look at the Princess Bree," he cried. "Not even swaying. That's one powerful tolerance."

I neglected to mention my temperance had something to do with it.

"Of course, Halflings are always more powerful than normal fairies," he added, laughing.

"Oh really?" I turned to Kian, who glowered. "You didn't mention that, Kian."

"'Course they are!" said Pan, giggling, oblivious to Kian's black stares. "Simple evolution. Most humans die of a fairy kiss; only the strong ones survive. So any halfies – they're made of some pretty strong stuff. Simple evolution."

"Is this true, Kian?"

He said nothing. At last he conceded the point. "I didn't think it, ah, politic to remind my... guest...

that she was particularly powerful, under the circumstances."

I shot him a honeyed smile. "Of course not," I said. "I understand *completely.*"

I didn't want to admit, but I was enjoying our repartee. Mortal enemy or not, Kian could match me word for word and raised eyebrow for raised eyebrow; there was a reason, I thought, that we were both of royal blood. And by the laws of magic were each other's intended. It was certainly better than being attacked by Pixies.

Once we got to the Winter Court, I thought, we'd be able to work this out. I had been in Model UN at school, after all; how different could fairy politics be? I was sure the war between the Winter and Summer Courts could be ended with the right amount of royal influence – and I was the Crown Princess. And then, I thought, against myself, the marriage contract would still be on.

I looked up at Kian – who seemed even more beautiful by candlelight than he had some hours earlier – and pushed the thought out of my mind. It was just the fairyfruit wine, I decided.

Pan, meanwhile, had taken to dancing on the table. He had captured what looked like a firefly in his palms, and placed it under a clear glass vase; thus trapped, the firefly began to sing, a plaintive melody.

"He's asking us to let him go," said Pan. "It's the ballad-bug's custom!"

"You can't imprison a living creature!" I said. I shot a look at Kian for emphasis.

"Excuse me," said Pan, "but it's tradition, Princess. Ballad-bug sings us a song in order to gain his freedom, we let it go; it flies around happily until the next guy gets him. We'll give it some fairyfruit wine before it goes. It doesn't mind."

Fair enough, I thought. The ballad-bug's song didn't seem too miserable – he struck up a rather jazzy note, and soon Pan had leapt to his feet to dance some more.

"Come on, have a go, Princess," cried Pan, taking my hands in his. He smelled like goat, only less pleasant.

"I'd rather not," I said.

"Well, if you'd rather go somewhere more private," continued Pan, yanking me around the small living room floor. "We can go upstairs and have a little... party of our own!"

"That's... very flattering," I said, "but I must protest."

"Just a kiss?" continued Pan. "Come one, just one!"

"That's enough!" cried Kian. "You are talking to a princess of royal fairy blood! Summer or Winter court, I won't have any lady of her rank and blood be maligned by insolent advances! Go upstairs and lie down – that's a royal command!"

Pan didn't seem to be in any mood to assent, but apparently a royal command had some magical component; almost against himself, Pan was carried upwards, up the stone staircase, and out of view.

"I apologize, Your Highness," said Kian. The deference was real this time. "War or no war, there are honorable ways to behave."

"Tradition," I said, releasing the ballad-bug. It blew me a kiss with a tiny, puckered mouth before dipping its wings in the jug of fairyfruit wine and flying off. "Of course." I couldn't help but soften. "Thank you," I said.

"I didn't mean to... behave with disrespect in taking you prisoner," Kian continued. "It was nothing personal."

"Oh, of course," I said. "You're only my ex-intended."

"That wasn't my choice," Kian said quietly. "I did not decide to go to war. But I must do my duty by my kingdom, and if that means giving up... my intended, then I must." He blushed, slightly. "Whatever the laws of magic might say to the contrary."

"I thought there was no law stronger than that of magic," I said above a whisper.

He looked up at me, his eyes darker and more intense. "There is no law stronger than that of magic," he said softly. He was standing perilously close to me; his hair shimmered in the moonlight. At that moment, I could believe what he said was true. We were standing close enough where I can see my reflection in his eyes and if I lifted my hand, I could easily trace the soft curve of his full lips with my fingertips. He half-closed his eyes and reached his arms around me, gathering me closer. I half-closed my eyes... anticipating what I had always dreamed about.

"I must to bed," he said harshly, suddenly pulling himself away. "I suggest you get some rest. In the morning, Princess, we head to the Winter Court. You can sleep on the divan; I'm afraid it would be unseemly to allow you into my private quarters upstairs. Can I trust you to not run away – if I don't tie you up, I mean," he seemed rather embarrassed.

"I give you my word as a Princess," I said, trying not to think about Kian's arms around me just seconds ago.

"Then I will trust you – as any chivalric Prince ought to do. Goodnight."

I curled up on the divan and went to sleep – too tired to reflect any longer on this long, strange day.

Chapter 8

The dawn woke me before Kian did. It was a strange dawn, so unlike the sunrises in my world. First, a deep red light was cast over the mountainside – I thought at first that some creatures had set the woods aflame, for in the human world the only light that makes that color is fire. Then it faded into orange, a ripe, juicy color, before gradually turning into the bright, golden yellow that we in human-land associate only with summer days at noon– those rare, stolen hours on beaches, or in meadows, when the world seems as balmy and warm and delightful as a golden retriever's fur.

I began to understand, and was not surprised when the light slowly turned green – a soft, melting color like the color of the fairy trees, and then blue, indigo, and purple – the colors of a rainbow. I was, however, surprised when red came again, faster this time, and then the cycle repeated, each time getting faster and faster until there was nothing but rainbow light in all its gleaming manifestations cast about the floor of the little lodge.

"Oh, my head..." I could hear Pan moaning from upstairs. I had to admit I felt a little sorry for him. Plenty of boys at my high school got drunk and did stupid things, but they very rarely had the anger of a royal Prince to contend with afterwards.

I continued staring at the fairy dawn, entranced by the sparkling sunlight. I peeked my head out of the window to see what would happen next. Everything in this world was so new, so wonderful and strange – like things in my old world, but better. I always used to imagine that I didn't – "fit" in human world, that there was something wrong, that I as meant to be somewhere else and it was only by some accident in providence that I was a sixteen-year-old girl with scuffed shoes and my hair in a ponytail poring over Algebra homework. And now I had found my answer. For sixteen years my soul had been drawn towards this place, this alien homeland, towards its rainbow sunrises and whispering trees.

It was almost worth it, I couldn't help thinking – to risk my life with pixies and minotaurs alike, if it meant seeing a sunrise like this.

The sun – a great blazing mass – began to separate. One sun was orange and yellow, fiery and extraordinary, with tongues of hot flame leaping out. It settled far in the distance, in a piece of the sky that was bright and blue and vivid. The other sun was smooth and milky – like an egg, even like what in the old world would have been called a moon – and it settled among the white expanses right above us, providing a gleaming, bluish light.

"Two suns here," said Kian, coming up behind me so softly, my heart jumped. "The Winter Sun and the Summer Sun."

"So, my kingdom's over there?" I said, pointing at the blazing orange ball in the distance.

"Yes," he said. "That is the land of Summer."

I felt pride seeping into my heart. "I like it better than this sun," I said. "I've always liked summer better than winter."

"As is fitting," said Kian. "I do apologize I cannot escort you to your homeland. It is my hope that… you will arrive there eventually."

"It's fine," I said. "You're doing what you have to do. I'm sure once we explain to the Winter Queen it'll all get sorted out. We'll get Shasta home, and then I can come myself.."

"I hope so," said Kian. His face was dark; his eyes seemed full of shadows. For a very brief moment, I thought I saw him tensed a little, as though he wanted to do something, but thought against it.

We set out that morning up the mountain into which Kian's hunting lodge had been carved. The snow was not bitter; the cold was not painful. Rather, the flurries were gentle on my skin, like soft balls of cotton, and the wind was not sharp and biting but only invigorating – filling me with cool, fresh energy as my hair blew into the wind.

"So, tell me more about Feyland," I said to Kian. "While we walk. I want to know everything about it!"

"I was never very good at history lessons when I was a boy," said Kian. "I always found them very dull."

"Well, I don't find it dull," I said. "I liked history when I was at school" – and I think Feyland history is even more interesting than the normal kind."

"To be fair," said Kian, "for me, this is the normal kind. Names and dates and Fairy Kings and Queens and Fairy Wars."

"Make it interesting," I pleaded. "Start it with "once upon a time.""

Kian laughed. "Isn't that what your type says when starting 'fairy stories?' "

"Yes! Do you tell human stories here?"

"Sometimes. They're usually..." He flushed a bit, his white ears turning pink. "Well, they're usually a bit rude" – the sort of tales one tells in a pub. The denizens of Feyland find the absence of magic to be quite funny. I mean no offense."

"None taken."

"For example – In the Land Over the Crystal River (for that's how we refer to humans), there was once a man and a woman. And the man was in love with the woman, and wanted her for himself. But because he had no magic, he couldn't feel whether or not there was a "pull" towards her or not, so he didn't know whether she loved him or not. So what did he do?"

"What?"

"He had to ASK her!" Kian couldn't help laughing.

"I don't get it!"

"Ask her!" said Kian. "It's funny – because he didn't have magic." His laughter grew louder and less controlled, tinkling like bells in the winter snow. "He had to ask her!"

I realized that there were some cultural barriers Kian and I might never transcend.

"So how does one get from human land to Feyland?"

"It's not geographic," said Kian. "It's magic. And the greatest magic of all lies along the Crystal River. Which is why people go there" – to use magic – and get to the other side. Pixies do it now and then, for hunting, but really nobody bothers. It's difficult, exhausting, and – no offense – there really isn't much of interest out there."

"Fair enough," I said. "So how does magic work, anyway?"

Kian looked confused. "What do you mean?"

"Like" – what *is* it?"

He shook his head. "I've never thought about it," he said. "Magic just... is." He reflected. "Like, that stone over there. It's got a shape, right?"

"Yes."

"And it's got a size, and a weight," said Kian, "depending..."

"Sure," I said, wondering what physics had to do with it.

"Well, it's also got magic." Kian shrugged.

"And you have magic," I said.

"Everything has magic. But it's not all the same magic. And magic lets us do things – how can I put it? Connect with other magic things. So because I have magic, and the stone has magic, I enter into a relationship with the stone. And so, if I close my eyes..."

Suddenly, the stone started levitating.

"What did you do?"

"I don't know," said Kian. "That's magic. It's hard to explain. I asked it to get up, so it did. Or rather, it asked the air beneath it to push it up."

"But if you're fighting, say, a Pixie, you can't just ask it to die?"

"That would be stupid," snorted Kian. "You ask your sword to find the heart" – you ask the skin on the Pixie's body to split open" (I felt a bit sick at that) "You ask a stone to trip up the Pixie. And the Pixie asks his sword, his stones, and so on to do the same to you. The stronger the magic, the more likely the rest of Feyland is to obey you."

I reflected. It seemed sensible. "So are there just two kingdoms?" I asked.

"In Feyland," said Kian, "There are two fairy kingdoms" – Summer and Winter. There used to be Autumn and Spring as well, but they've been conquered – they're now more like vassals, or city-states. Spring is the vassal of Summer, and Autumn is the vassal of Winter."

"And you don't have seasons, like we do."

"Not like you do," said Kian.

"So how do you mark the passage of time?"

"The Crystal River's tide," said Kian. "It overflows the bank about once every one hundred separations of the sun, which is like dawn to you lot."

"And is that how you mark years?"

"More or less."

I tried to calculate in my head. Assuming separating of the suns happened once every human day, there would be three and a half fairy-years, give or take, in every human year. "So I'm about sixty fairy years old," I said.

"Yes – the marriageable age," said Kian.

We heard a rustling in the leaves.

"What's that?" I asked, my hand clenching around the dagger Kian had given me.

"Stand with your back to mine," said Kian. "If someone attacks, ask the dagger to hit home."

The leaves rustled again. I drew the dagger.

"Breena!" came a familiar voice. It was Logan.

"Logan!" I cried, rushing to him. "You're alive!"

"No thanks to your friend," said Logan, snarling.

He looked different in Feyland. His figure was still human, but now, more than ever before, I could see the wolf in him.

"How did you get here?"

"With difficulty," Logan said. "I'll explain later." He turned to Kian. "Would you mind letting her go, please, so I can escort the Princess to the Summer Court, where she belongs?"

"This is an affair of state," said Kian, testily.

"Werewolves have no political allegiance," said Logan. "I am not bound by fairy laws or fairy contracts."

"I have no time to deal with the landless right now," said Kian. "I have to escort her to the Winter Court."

"You can get me to the Summer Court?" I cut in. "You know where it is?"

"Look, Bree," said Logan. "Werewolves – the– *landless* – as Kian insists on calling us – we go back and forth between the worlds. Half in human, half in Feyland... I know Feyland well."

I stepped towards Logan. I had been fine going to the Winter Court as long as there was no viable alternative; under the circumstances, however, I would much rather go home.

Kian drew his sword. "I cannot allow you to remove her from my presence," said Kian. "Furthermore," he added, "Bree has sworn a fairy oath to stay with me."

"You did *what*?" Logan reared up.

"Look, Logan..."

There was no time to explain. Logan began a low, low, howl – the vibrations coursing through his body, his body which was changing, subtly and yet so quickly...

The wolf jumped onto Kian.

"Wait, stop!" I cried. We were still in the middle of a dangerous mountainside, and the last thing I wanted was two wounded allies who couldn't protect each other or me.

Kian fought back, reaching for his dagger, his wings flapping beneath his cloak, sprays of silver falling onto the ground.

"Stop it!" I cried again. "I'm not going anywhere, so you can quit wasting time!"

"Oh, yes you are," said a voice in my ear.

I knew it all too well.

It was the Pixie.

Chapter 9

✳

I knew Delano's voice. It was cold, and cruel; it chilled my veins like ice water. I could feel his icy breath upon the back of my neck, feel his sharp, bony fingers enclose around my wrists.

"Sorry to interrupt," said Delano. "But I'm feeling particularly hungry right now."

Kian and Logan had broken apart, and were now both facing me, panting, covered in blood. I knew better than they did that they were in no state to protect me now. I tried to grab my dagger, but it was no use. Delano's hands were tight around mine, forcing my arms around my back.

Magic, I thought. I tried asking the dagger to come to me, but to no avail. It remained firm in my belt.

"Let's get rid of this, shall we?" Delano grabbed the dagger from my waist and tossed it aside in the bushes.

"Let her go, Pixie," cried Kian, "or you will have the wrath of the Winter Kingdom upon you."

"I'm a pixie," said Delano. "I already have the wrath of both Winter and Summer upon me, and I don't intend to stop now. If you know what's good for you, you'll allow me to claim my prize."

Logan howled.

"Come any closer and I'll kill her now," said Delano. "But I'd rather you didn't. I prefer to dine at home. In private."

I shuddered.

Kian and Logan were too far away, now. There was nothing they could do. I could not struggle, and I hated myself for my uselessness. I hadn't even been able to hold onto my dagger.

"Time to sleep, Breena," said Delano. He leaned into my ear and whispered something – some strange, hissing words that I could not understand. Suddenly everything started spinning around me– first Logan, who began flickering, turning back and forth into a wolf and a man, over and over again, and then the grass, which started changing color, and the sky – which went light and dark again and again.

"What's happening?" I tried to murmur, but no sound came out. There was only chaos – light and dark – swirling around me. The last thing I saw was Kian's face – the look of agony in his eyes as I started choking, fading, wilting...

And then everything went black.

I woke up in a dark room. The floor was wet with mold and slime; I could feel beneath me some carelessly tossed hay that I imagined was meant to be my bed. I couldn't see anything, only run my fingers up and down the rough stone, feel where it gave way to wood – a door! A locked door. I began to bang on the door.

"Let me out!" I cried. "You've made a mistake! You've gotten the wrong girl."

No answer. That wouldn't work. I tried again.

"I am the heir to the Summer throne. I am a fairy princess of the Summer court, and I order you to let me out!"

There came the sliding of metal, and a window in the door opened. Light came flooding into the room, stinging my eyes. A face popped into the window. I gasped. This was a pixie; I recognized it by the ears and the bony face, but unlike Delano this pixie wasn't beautiful. Rather, its face was contorted, savage, with a misshapen mouth and protruding hook nose, and a file of razor-sharp teeth lurking just beneath its fleshy lips.

"I don't take my orders from you, Princess," said the Pixie.

I tried to keep calm.

"How about bribes, then? Do you take those?"

The Pixie grinned at me.

"If you get me back to the Summer Court," I said, "You will be richly rewarded. I will give you gold – silver – treasures beyond measure. Think how much fairyfruit wine that will buy."

"I can think of something I'd like to taste much, much more," said the Pixie, sneering at me. He sniffed. "Smells delicious."

"I am a Princess," I said. "At least let me speak to your leader! Do not leave me in this dungeon like some... some... common fairy!"

"Oh, don't worry," said the Pixie. "You were captured by the Pixie King, and he wants you all to himself."

I worried.

"That was the Pixie King?" I asked him.

"Poor princess. You'd be better off if it was one of us. King Delano likes to play with his food." The Pixie cackled; my blood froze.

I heard a voice, high and cold, entering the dungeons.

"Speaking to the prisoners, are we, Coller?"

"Just having a bit of fun," said the Pixie. I could hear the fear in his voice.

"For shame, Coller," said Delano. "That was a Princess of the Summer Court you were talking to."

"Some Princess," said Coller. "Just a fairy..."

"Show some respect, Coller. Princess, are you in there?"

My voice was shaking. "I'm there," I said, as bravely as I could.

"Good. Now, I do apologize for the behavior of my guard. Coller, I'm having you executed." He laughed.

"What? No.." Coller tried to protest.

"That's what happens when you disrespect a fairy of the royal Courts. Guards!"

I heard Coller's cries drowned out by the stamping of feet, the clanking of metal. There was an atrocious wail and then there was silence.

"You see, Princess; I don't tolerate disrespect in my court. Guards, let her out."

With a loud groan the door was opened. Delano appeared before me, clad now in what must have been royal pixie robes. His cloak was velvet, emerald green, setting off the eerie light in his neon eyes.

"Your Highness," he bowed and kissed my hand.

"Your Highness," I said back to him. My legs were too wobbly for me to attempt a curtsey.

"I do apologize for these dreadful conditions. I'm afraid our guest quarters are not up to the same standard as the rest of the palace. Won't you come with me?"

He took my hand, and for a moment I let my guard down. Then I felt his sharp nails digging into my palm and I once again began to feel afraid.

He took me out of the dungeons and led me down a long passageway. I could feel the magic inhabiting the place, but this was not like the magic of the fairy courts – alive, intense, and vital. This magic was as still, even stagnant, hanging off the Gothic archways, the empty suits of armor, and the stones.

Delano led me into a sumptuous antechamber. Everything was silver, except for the throne, which was studded with green gemstones. The design was exquisite and terrifying – as I stared, I thought I could hear the stones screaming, each one crying out in agony, its magic vibrating as it tried to rip itself out of the chair.

"I see you admire the furnishings," said Delano. "That's Classical King Illyrium Style – about three thousand years old – a masterpiece of the design. Characterized by torturing the gemstones – that scream you hear is part of the design. It's a bit unsettling for visitors to the Pixie realm. Not that many survive to tell the tale, of course."

"Are you going to eat me?" I asked him.

I thought perhaps it was better to get that niggling uncertainty out of the way.

"Well, if you insist..." Delano laughed.

"Not particularly," I said.

"Why would I eat you?" said Delano.

"Don't you suck the blood of humans and fairies?"

"Well, *some*," said Delano. "But not important ones. Not fairies like you. And you're a Halfling, after all – which makes you extra rare, extra special! Why would I waste you on a meal?"

"I wouldn't encourage it," I said.

"I've got much better plans in store for you," said Delano.

I wondered if he wanted to exchange me to the Summer Court, too.

"Half-human, half-fairy. The most powerful combination. You have the magic of fairyland, but the life-force of the land Beyond the Crystal River – fertility, strength, passion. All qualities lacking in most fairies," he continued. "What a race you could produce. Part-fairy, part-human," he looked up at me and smiled. "Part-Pixie."

"I wasn't planning on breeding anytime soon," I said.

"You're of age, aren't you? Don't worry – I'm not trying to insult you. I don't intend to possess you and toss you aside, like one of the concubines of the Summer Court."

I tried very hard not to focus on the fact that one of those concubines had been my mother.

"I want to marry you," he said. "Make you my Queen. Produce a new race – the strongest race that Feyland has ever seen. Of course, Feyland is rather a misnomer," he added. "The fairies named this place, and certainly didn't bother asking us. Perhaps you can think of a better name for it, Breena? In the Pixie-language, we call it Skirnismor – Country of the Pixies. The part the fairies rule is Skirnifellentru – The Land the Fairies Stole."

"I see," I said.

"You could be Queen," said Delano. "Queen of two kingdoms. The Summer Court, and the Pixie Lands."

"That would make you King of the Summer Court."

"Oh yes. Eventually. Upon the death of the incumbent."

"My father?"

Delano laughed. "Silly girl. The Summer King is a pathetic wisp of a man. Everyone knows the court is ruled in truth by the Summer Queen. So, you see – it is in your interest to depose her. She is not even any relation of yours. She is only standing between you and the greatest power in Skirnismor."

I wanted to buy time, to figure out what was going on. I certainly wasn't prepared to marry a pixie – or anyone else, for that matter – but nor was I keen to be eaten alive by one of Coller's companions. – "It's certainly a tempting offer," I said. "But forgive me – how can I possibly give you an answer under these conditions?"

"What do you mean?"

"I need time to think it over." I said.

"Well, it's rather an easy choice. You can marry me, and become my queen, or you can become my concubine and bear my children illegitimately." He shrugged. "The stigma here is the same as it is in your world. Your mother, for example, is considered just as much of a whore in Skirnismor as she must be in Gregory, Oregon."

"How dare you!" I shouted, losing my self-control for the moment.

"Halfling or not – you are still a bastard child," he continued. "Unable to hold any real power in the Summer Court until the Summer Queen's death. There is no place in Skirnismor that will protect you, Breena. Find your own protection. Rule Skirnismor."

I understood my decision. Either I was to marry Delano, giving him rights over the Summer Court in exchange for relative freedom and power as Pixie Queen, or I was to succumb to his advances another way – producing valuable heirs, perhaps, but nevertheless trapped, without any power of my own, in the Pixie castle. Neither plan sounded particularly appealing.

I remembered laughing with Logan one day, not long ago, about romance. – "I'll probably die a virgin," I had said to him, bemoaning my lack of romance. "Then again, that's better than going out with one of the football jocks." How long ago that life seemed! The idea of bearing children to a pixie disgusted me. I had never even been kissed.

"I'll need to consider the matter," I said.

Delano laughed. "Take all the time you need. However – if we're not to be married, I'm afraid I cannot – how can I put this – host you in my private quarters. Propriety, you understand. You'll have to go back to the – ahem – guest rooms. I'll come to see you tomorrow – perhaps you'll give me an answer then."

And with that, two guards seized me, and dragged me back into the dungeon.

I could not sleep that night. I sat, rocking back and forth, trying to decide what to do. I had no doubt that Delano would have no compunctions about forcing himself upon me in order to produce an heir – that as a concubine I would be little more than a slave, and yet I could not bring myself to agree to be his Queen, to consent to the terrible situation that had been forced upon me. There was nobody in Feyland I could trust – the Summer Kingdom seemed not to want me, the Winter Kingdom wanted to take me prisoner, the pixies wanted to use me as some kind of human breeding machine.

I remembered my dreams, how I had so longed to go back to fairyland. I felt now that perhaps it would have been better if I had just stayed in Gregory after all.

Chapter 10

✳

The night seemed to last forever – if it was night at all. There were no windows in the dungeon, and I had no way of knowing how long I was there, how long the time went. I remembered Jared Dushev, whom the pixies had bitten, and who had gone mad. But now I began to think that the pixies didn't need to bite anyone to make them mad – no, they could drive a person crazy just by locking them in here. I curled up on my bed of hay and tried to decipher what it was I should do next. I had no weapons, no magic, and Logan and Kian were probably miles and miles away. Even if I were to escape, I had no idea how to get home to the mortal realm – beyond the Crystal River was a rather vague description at best – and I certainly didn't stand a chance of getting there before being eaten by minotaurs, captured by pixies, or arrested by the Winter Court. Kian had been kind to me, despite his duty to his home kingdom, but I remembered Flynn, and Pan the satyr, and I couldn't help but feel sure that many of the other winter fairies wouldn't be so kind. The Summer Court didn't seem like much help, either – I had hoped that, as heiress to the throne, I might hold some sort of power, but it seemed that as long as the Summer Queen held the real power in the kingdom, I could no longer rely on her. Which left me, I realized, with Delano. I had no means of escape, after all, and so my choices were few; either I could remain a prisoner and, most likely, a concubine of the Pixie King, breeding half-breed children that would be taken away from me before I could even catch a glimpse of them, rotting away in these miserable walls, or I could become a Pixie Queen. I remembered the screaming emeralds in the throne, the horrible magic of Pixie crafts, and I shuddered. Plus, if I married Delano, he would have rights over the Summer Court. Neither choice seemed anything but terrible to me.

If I only had more time...

I tried to remember what Kian had told me about magic. *Ask the stone to move.* If everything was magic, here, and if I was magic, too, then surely this meant that I could learn to somehow connect with these unearthly things.

I needed to start small. I grabbed a decidedly unmagical-looking piece of hay and placed it before me. I closed my eyes, trying to feel my magic, the way I could feel my weight, my height, my place in space. I didn't feel anything. I tried to concentrate harder, thinking of moments that made me feel powerful, feel special, feel that there was magic running alongside the blood in my veins. I remembered my dreams, the gorgeous palaces and cloud-capped towers of the Summer Court, the whispering willows and juicy orange-vines in the garden; I remembered the fairy waltz. I tried to recall its music – that strange and melodic sound that sounded like no other music in the world, because it was magic that made the instruments play – the magic of the musician connecting with the magic in the object.

I thought of the dance, of the steps. I stared at the stalk of hay, trying to find the magic inside of it, trying to get closer...

Somewhere, in the back of my mind, I saw Kian's face, as it had been in my dreams, night after night – the proud and icy-eyed knight of the Winter Kingdom, felt his lips pressing close to mine, felt him lean down, saw myself reflected in his eyes...

I gave into the feeling. At once I felt a strange sensation – like heat, but not heat – like cold, but not cold. My body was running hot and cold, at once, as if I had a fever, and then hotter and hotter, so hot I could hardly stand it, so hot that I imagined I would burn up and still my temperature kept rising. I pressed a hand to my forehead; it was as cool as it had always been. Where was the feeling coming from?

I felt a rush of energy leave my body; in the dark of the room, I could see the faintest glimmer as the piece of hay leaped into the air, making a spiral, before sinking down into the ground.

Well, it was a start.

I practiced with the hay for what seemed like days. I had not eaten; I had not slept. I only tried to get the hay to do my bidding – to contort into shapes, to move around, to change color. I tried to work similar magic on the doors of the prison, but

I felt an automatic push against me when I tried, a sudden, jolting pain in my forehead. If the doors had magic, I reasoned, it had been already enchanted to repel me.

At one point the guards opened the window and threw me a crust of bread.

"Let us know when you're ready to talk to Delano," said one of the guards.

I could see the key jingling in the pockets of Flaurmaus, who had replaced Coller as my primary guard. He, perhaps more wisely than his predecessor, did not speak to me. I tried to magic the key in my general direction; it, like the door, had been magicked.

The case seemed hopeless. Moving bits of hay and bread around was all very well and good, but it would do me little benefit against the Pixie Delano and his whole terrifying army.

Until I realized something else. I could move hay; I could move bread. I could change its color, its size (useful, I realized, when I was hungry), and its weight.

But what if I could also change its shape?

The next time the guards brought me bread, I didn't eat anything. Instead, I stared through the little window at Flaurmaus's keychain – at the precise size and shape of the key, how it looked, how it fit into the lock. I tried to use my magic to save a picture of it in my mind.

I stared at the bread, willing it to morph itself into a reproduction of the key, willing it to grow harder – staler – until it had calcified.

By the time the guards next came around for my feeding, I had succeeded in turning half my bread into a key, the other half into small, dense, hard balls – as heavy and solid as lead.

I had to think quickly. I concentrated on the balls first, willing them to attack the guard, to strike him directly between the eyes. He went down immediately. I scanned the hallway for signs of another guard – nobody was there – I magicked the key through the hole and down into the lock; the door swung open. The key, straining under the effort (for deep down, it really was bread), at last broke in half, dissolving into crumbs on the floor. Not a moment too soon, I thought.

And then I saw the locked door at the end of the hall.

"Bree!" I heard a familiar voice – warm and reassuring – and looked up to see two guards rushing towards me. I froze.

"It's us."

Beneath the armor of the Pixie guards I could make out the faces of Logan and Kian.

"Are you all right?" I could see Kian's frown beneath his visor.

"I'm fine – we'll talk later. How did you get in?"

"How did you get *out*?" Logan cut in.

Kian cut him off. "We found some guards on patrol outside the castle; knocked them out and replaced them."

"Hold on," I said, turning back to the guard I had knocked out. "Think these will fit me?"

I hurriedly put on the Pixie chain mail, sticking the visor over my face. I took the keys out of the guard's pocket for good measure.

"We'll talk later," said Kian. "For now, let's get out of here."

We tried our best to look like three Pixie soldiers on patrol. For a few, brilliant moments, we thought we had succeeded. We were able to exit the dungeons and make our way to the Great Hall. We nodded curtly to the other soldiers, hiding our faces beneath our visors.

And then the magic alarm went off.

It was a silent alarm; nevertheless we could sense it, hear it in our bones, a sick, strange feeling that meant *something is wrong in the castle*, and we saw that the Pixies could see it too.

They rounded on us. "Them!" called one of them.

"It's the Princess!" cried another, more clear-sighted.

Kian and Logan drew their swords. "We're outnumbered," Kian called. "Prepare to fight to the death," he said to Logan. There was a casual kind of honor in his voice; to die for a cause afforded him little terror. His self-control was chilling. It was the noblest thing I had ever seen.

Logan seemed a bit less willing to die. He tore into the Pixies madly, hacking them with his sword. I stood behind them, with my back against the wall, as they fended off pixie after pixie. If only there was something I could do...

I caught sight of the chandelier and focused on it, trying to concentrate amid the din of the fighting. It was harder than doing magic in the dungeon – the object was bigger, and I didn't have the time to concentrate. I tried only to shut my eyes and feel the fairy waltz in my bones, think of Kian, think of his lips on mine, feel the magic bubbling up out of me.

It rocked; it swayed.

Just a little bit harder, I thought (and in my imagination Kian's lips had pressed against mine; my mouth was opening; I could feel his hands tight against my back...)

The rope holding up the chandelier snapped, and the candelabras crashed down into a hoard of Pixie soldiers. It was just enough of a distraction to let us cross the Great Hall, towards the gate, towards the bridge across the moat, which was rapidly being closed by a series of sentries...

In the din, Logan and I had become separated from Kian, who was fending off ten Pixie soldiers at once.

He turned and hissed at us. "Go!" he said.

I hesitated.

"Go, Princess!"

I saw at last the sword fly out of his hand, saw the Pixie soldiers descend upon him, twining chains around his arms.

Logan grabbed me. "Get on my back."

I didn't have time to think. I leaped onto his shoulders, and landed on the firm, taut, muscular back of a wolf, digging my fingers deep into his fur, holding on as tightly as I could...

He began running at an unearthly speed, his hindquarters shaking the ground. The bridge was closing, closing...

With every ounce of magic I had left, I willed it to stay open for just a moment longer...

He took the bridge at one great, terrible run. I could feel the wind on our faces as we leaped through the sky, over the moat, out of the castle. The wolf that had been Logan kept running, until at last I could feel in the air that there were no pixies following us.

He stopped, and let me roll off his back.

And there we were. Alone, in the night, with no idea where we were going, where to go, if anyone was following us. The two of us – alone.

And Kian was back in the Pixie castle, weighed down with chains, the prisoner of Delano, King of the Pixies.

They said Delano liked to play with his food.

Chapter 11

✳

We stood alone in the darkness. The wind whipped around us, and even the stars were terrifying, for with every faint and unearthly glow that came out of the endless night my heart tightened and I thought again of the Pixies following us, with their misshapen faces, their glowing eyes, their cruel mouths.

"Where do we go now," I said to Logan. I didn't have time to think about anything but survival; there was a great stone inside my throat, an overwhelming emptiness overtaking me.

He placed an arm around me. "I know this place," he said. "In the forest. It's an outpost of the werewolves – a cave. We'll go there. Get on my back." He transformed again – first his ears and hands and feet, then the rest of him– and I got on top of him. The smell of his fur reassured me – the same musty, familiar Logan-smell that always used to remind me of the woodlands outside Gregory High School.

By the time we reached the cave, I was shaking.

Logan transformed back into a man, and began looking for sticks of wood. "Here," he said. "Start rubbing these together – see if you can get them to light."

I tried to use magic, to imagine the fairy waltz as I had back in the Pixie castle, but every time I thought of Kian my blood turned to ice; I could not do it. Fat, throbbing tears dripped down onto the wood.

"We'll have to do it the normal way," said Logan.

At last the fire was lit. But this was not normal fire. Instead of burning brightly, it seemed to obscure the rest of Feyland – the trees and shadows that we saw outside the cave entrance turned into endless black, while somehow the shapes and figures in the cave itself seemed perfectly clear. "It's darkfire," said Logan. "The Pixies won't see anything beyond this point – even if they look in the cave."

"Logan," I said at last. "What's going on?" My lips and chin were trembling. I was tired of being strong. I wanted to be a little girl again, a child, weak and protected; I wanted his arms around me, his comforting words. I wanted somebody else to tell me what to do. In the morning, maybe, I would be strong. Right now all I wanted to do was cry.

"Werewolves, we're not like other creatures," said Logan. "We're not magic in the same way. We're Halflings – real Halflings, not half-breeds like you. Half in the mortal world, half in this one. There's a legend about us – that a wolf fell into the Crystal River when he was just a cub, and that from that day on he needed to go back and forth into the mortal world and the magical one."

"I don't understand," I said.

"Our magic isn't the magic of Feyland – the cold, beautiful magic of fairy kings and queens. That magic, as you've learned, is often stifling; it's why so many fairies are barren – why whole royal lines are dying out, why the Summer Queen could not bear an heir. Magic is so strong, so powerful, that it overwhelms "normal life forces" – like procreation.

Fairies, pixies, and so forth don't need to eat in the way that humans or wolves do – in order to metabolize calories, to keep the heart pumping. What they eat energizes them magically – from fairyfruit wine to the blood of fairies. Werewolves are from the magical realm, but their power lies in the mortal life-force. We do not feed on blood or magic, nor on fairyfruit and magical plants and herbs – but on mortal food. So we must go back and forth..."

"And you never told me," I whispered.

"What could I say?" said Logan. "I was ashamed. I didn't know what you would think of me, Breena. So many times I had wanted to, but you were getting these dreams, and I didn't want to scare you. Werewolves are welcome in neither kingdom – they are seen as drifters, rogues, homeless vagabonds. Besides, how strange would such a thing sound? 'I'm a werewolf' You would have thought I was nuts."

"Did you know I was a fairy?"

He shook his head. "I knew you were special," he said. "But you would be special anyway, fairy princess or not. But I felt... a connection with you. I thought..." He sighed. "Never mind what I thought. The connection was because we both originated in the fairy kingdom – that's all." He looked angry for a moment.

"And so you've been living back and forth," I said. "Always?"

"Always."

"Then you must know how to get back!" I said. "How to get back to the mortal realm."

Logan nodded. "You made it easy," he said.

"What do you mean?"

"Your painting – in the art studio."

"My painting?"

"Have you ever seen fairy art?" Logan asked me.

I nodded, thinking of Kian's paintings in the hunting lodge, of the magic of the fairy waltz. The thought of Kian left a lump in my throat.

"It's the most magical thing there is," said Logan. "More magic goes into it than almost anything. Even your paintings of Kian – though you didn't know it – had magic in them. And that magic pulls you into fairyland."

I remembered Kian pulling me into the art studio before we arrived in Feyland, and understood.

"So, to get back, I just have to paint home?"

Logan shook his head. "Not that simple," he said. "You'll have to go to the Crystal River. It's far from here – as far as you can go. There are cliffs there – gorgeous cliffs, that look like limestone. And on those cliffs there are paintings – each painting the memory of a spell. And if you paint home there..."

"Is that what you did? Every day and night?"

"I told you," he said, "wolves don't have magic. For us, it's different. We can cross the Crystal River directly – just swim across – and find ourselves in the mortal world on the other side. We have a natural calling towards the mortal world that pulls us across."

"Can we get there?"

"Not easily," said Logan.

I could not ignore the lump in my throat any longer. At last I turned to Logan. "But what about Kian?"

His face darkened. "He was your captor," he said, "trying to sell you out to the Winter Court!"

"He was just honoring his kingdom!" I said. "He didn't mean it personally. It was... an affair of state."

Logan made a face. "That's just what he said," he said. "I didn't realize affairs of state made it okay to kidnap innocent girls."

"It was just a misunderstanding," I cried.

"You're awfully sympathetic," said Logan, "considering he left this massive gash in my arm." He pointed to where Kian had cut him with the sword.

"We can't just *leave* him there!" I said. "Delano will kill him."

"Probably," said Logan. "And then the Winter Court will be without an heir – a massive victory for the Summer Court."

"That's disgusting," I said.

"I thought it was just an affair of state!"

"Kian's not just some prince," I said.

"Oh, no, he's special!" Logan looked hurt and angry at the same time. "Bree..." his voice rising in frustration. "*I'm* here. You don't need Kian!"

I had never seen Logan like this before – I didn't like it.

"I don't see what you're being so petty about," I said. "Kian risked his life to save me from the Pixies. Both of you did. And I wouldn't leave either one of you behind."

"He risked his life to sell you out to the Winter Queen!"

"I owe him," I said, firmly. "And I'm going to go back." I didn't realize what I was going to say until I had said it. "And I'm going to rescue him."

"That's idiotic – how are you going to invade the Pixie Castle?"

"I can do magic," I said. "I did it in the cell"– I can lift things with my mind – cause them to change shape, size, color."

"So can all the Pixies."

"It's a question of honor," I said. "If I am a princess after all, then I'd better act like one. And I've read plenty of myths, Logan, and I don't know one where princes and princesses aren't meant to be honorable, brave, and strong."

"And stupid!" said Logan. "If you go back to the Pixie Castle alone you'll die."

"It's a question of honor," I said again.

"You sound like Kian," Logan scoffed.

"Well, I *am* like Kian," I said. "We're both fairies of the royal blood."

"Aren't you special?" said Logan. I could see the wolf in his eyes. "The Fairy Princess and the Fairy Prince. How perfect," he said sarcastically.

I got up. "If I do die," I said, "it's better than going back home as a coward." How could I go back home, anyway, after all I had seen? After all I had experienced? I thought of Gregory, Oregon, and nothing seemed further away. "And even if I go home, I won't be safe. Delano came last time; he'll come again. So I might as well fight for my friends."

"Bree – I'm sorry," said Logan. He reached out a hand. "I'm really sorry."

"Well, you should be," I snapped.

"You can't go alone," he said.

"I'll darn well go if I want to."

"You can go," he said. He slipped his hand in mine. "But then I'm going with you."

Chapter 12

We set out the following night. I had wanted to go out immediately, but Logan had spoken rationally to me. "If you want to go," he said, "Get some sleep first" – neither of us will be any use until we've cleaned up a little bit, washed out wounds, and had a bit of sleep. Otherwise we're just dead weight, and are more likely to get captured again than we are to free Kian. And we can't go during the day – Pixies will see us. No, we need to go under cover of the night. We'll wait until sundown."

Even my passion and worry were not enough to render me stupid; I agreed, albeit reluctantly, and tried to get some sleep, knowing that the more energy I had, the greater chance Kian had of surviving our attempted breakout. It was difficult. I spent the night tossing and turning with horrendous dreams. If before I had dreamed of Feyland while at home in my bed in Gregory, Oregon, then now I dreamed of home. I dreamed of my mother – could not imagine her pain, her terror, her fear when she came home to find the house broken into and her only daughter gone. Would she think it was a burglar, a kidnapper, a serial killer? Or would she be able to sense the fairy presence there! I dreamed of my mother, resplendent in a red gown, sitting on the fairy throne with a faceless, nameless Summer King. She was flirting with him, letting him kiss her neck, laughing.

I tried to call out to her, ask her for help against the Summer and Winter Queens, against the Pixies, but it was no use. She ignored my pleas and my plaintive cries. – "Can't you see I'm busy?" she said, and reclined her head into the Summer King's chest. "Go play elsewhere! I'm on a date!"

Then I dreamed of Logan, the Logan I had known since I could remember, he and I playing chase as children through the woods near my house, his handsome familiar face laughing with joy, his warm eyes always reassuring, his arms always there to hug me and envelope me with his musky woodsy scent whenever Clariss or another bully harassed me. Suddenly his arms became longer, his hands widen, his fingers extended into razor-sharp claws, and fur the color of Logan's hair ran up and down his arms ending at the tip of his tail. His tail? When did Logan have a tail? A voice at the back of my dream-state mind asked, perhaps trying to reason with my now present state that Logan has become, has always been a werewolf. He had always known of Feyland, the Feyland of my dreams… of Kian, the Winter Prince when I had only thought it was a dream. While pouring out the details of my dream, rather embarrassingly to Logan, all these years, capturing the memories unto canvas in my paintings, Logan had always known that this Feyland, this strange, but wondrously beautiful land, was real.

And the emeralds were there, the emeralds of the Pixie Court, each gemstone screaming in agony, tortured by magic. Their screams grew louder and louder, filling my ears, filling the space between my thoughts, and the pain grew greater and greater – for I was feeling the pain too – until at last everything went black.

I dreamed next of Kian, lying in the dank dungeons of the Pixie King, his silver blood soaking into the bales of hay, the manic eyes of Flaurmaus and the other guards upon him, Delano's cruel teeth contorting into a smile...

And in my dream I saw his face – the silvery eyes, flecked with purple quartz, the creamy skin, the long black hair – and I felt that my soul had already gone to him, already fought off the Pixie guards and the Minotaurs and the dangers and terrors of the forest. I was asleep in the werewolf-cave, but it didn't matter. My soul, the truest, most sacred part of myself, was already with Kian. All I had to do was follow it.

Waiting until sundown was the hardest part. I grew skittish and nervous; I bothered Logan a hundred times as I tapped my foot on the floor, my fingers on the walls of the cave. The tension in the air between us was overwhelming. I could not understand why he was so loath to save Kian, who had after all been my protector, if a rather reluctant one, during my time in fairyland. At the same time I saw the look of jealousy and spite in his eyes, the resentment whenever I mentioned Kian's name, and I realized that I knew the cause of his tetchiness – I did not want to know. I remembered the day of my sixteenth birthday – so long ago now– when Logan and I had run around the house, chasing each other with the canisters of whipped cream. He had helped me wash the sticky mess out of my hair, had wiped it from my cheek and stared into my eyes – we had been so close to…

But that was before Kian. That was before the forests of Feyland, before I had learned to do magic, before I had been captured by a pixie, before the Minotaurs and the satyrs and summer and winter. It was before I had felt Kian's arms around me.

He knew why I was silent; I knew why he was silent.

At sundown we set out for the Pixie Castle again.

Logan had transformed once more into a wolf; I rode on his back, wrapping his long, flowing fur around my fingers to keep my balance. He was sleek and stealthy in the night, his paws quieter than the breeze as they lightly pushed up against the grass. The wind whipped our cheeks; the moon was huge and luminous above us – a circle of whiteness cut out from the endless night.

At last we saw the Pixie Castle in the distance. This was the first time I'd looked at it properly – during our escape we'd been so frantic to get out of there that we hadn't bothered to look back. The sight made me gasp. The stones were thick and dark, laid over with shining black quartz, so that the whole castle reflected the night – the inky blackness surrounding it. But the towers! Each tower – and there must have been ten or twenty of them – took the form of a spiral staircase. But they were not made of stone. Rather, they were made of some strange, grotesque gauzy material – nauseating, twitching, weak-colored gossamer that shook under the weight of each Pixie guard on control. At the end of each piece of gossamer there lay a throbbing chunk of what must have been flesh, stained with sticky silver.

Fairy wings.

Hundreds, if not thousands of fairies had been slaughtered here; their wings had been ripped out of their back and affixed to thick metal poles, creating the fluttering, twitching spiral staircases. When I was little, I had seen one of my classmates – a boy called Charles Janeway – torture butterflies, capturing them and sticking pins in their wings and laughing gleefully when they strained and strangled against his cruelty. It had made me feel sick, then, and I had rushed into some corner of my kindergarten classroom to cry. This was a hundred times worse.

"Right," I said. "Let's go on, then."

"They'll be expecting us," said Logan.

We could not masquerade as pixies again; since our break-in, we were sure they would be on the lookout.

We had another plan.

I used my magic to transform Logan's face into the wintry expression of a fairy prince of the Winter Court, and transformed some of the blades of grass into chains. I had not expected to be quite as good at transfiguring faces as I had been – but in the end it was easy. I only had to picture Kian's face – and everything I tried to transfigure, somehow, took Kian's expression.

Logan wrapped the chains around my wrist, leaving a loophole for me to pull my wrists out if necessary, and we entered the Pixie Castle by the front gates.

"Hark," he said. "I am Snowshadow of the Winter Court, and I have returned with bounty from the Winter Court in exchange for the Princess Breena."

I pretended to struggle and yelp.

"I demand an audience with Delano, King of the Pixies."

"And why shouldn't we just grab her here and now?" asked one of the guards. I recognized him from earlier.

"Because," said Logan. In a flash, he had put a knife to my throat. "If you don't, I'll kill her now – and a dead Halfling is much less use to your king than a living, breathing one. Dead Halflings don't bear children."

The guard nodded.

I shuddered; it was a good thing they had not decided to call Logan's bluff.

The guards led us into Delano's antechamber, which was all too familiar.

"Well," said Delano. "Well done."

"I come from the Winter Court," said Logan. "I am the knight Snowshadow. I wish to exchange the Prince Kian for Princess Breena."

Delano considered.

"My guards tell me you have threatened to kill Breena should I refuse the exchange."

Logan nodded curtly.

"Impressive show – for a fairy. Bring out the Prince!"

The guards dragged in Kian. He had been beaten – his face and body were covered with silver bruises. My heart leaped when I saw him.

"Princess" – you've run away…"

I decided to feign terror. "Please don't kill me!" I said. "I'll be your wife – I'll be your Queen – only just don't kill me!"

Kian's eyes blazed with anger. "You!" he cried to Logan. "Knight of the Court! How dare you act so dishonorably to a woman! I shall have you executed at once when I am freed!"

Logan could resist. "Come now, Prince," he said. "Did you yourself not capture the Princess to trade her to the Summer Court?"

"I would have returned her to her rightful home!" cried Kian.

Calm down, I thought. *Kian, it's all right.*

I don't know how it worked, but I saw Kian's shoulders slump; his expression became more relaxed. He had heard me.

"Unhand him," said Delano, and the guards removed Kian from his chains and shoved him forth. Logan kicked me down to Delano's knees; I began causing a distraction, wrapping my hands around Delano's ankles and blubbering, begging for mercy, promising to marry him.

In the meantime, obscured by my histrionics, Logan handed Kian a sword...

"Now!" Logan shouted, and immediately I loosened myself from my chains, retrieving a dagger I had hidden in my skirts and holding it up to Delano's neck, focusing all my magic, all my energy, on keeping in there.

I heard a powerful flapping sound as Kian unleashed his wings – thank God they hadn't cut them off yet, I thought.

"Don't move," I cried out to the guards, digging my dagger a bit further into Delano's neck. His blood was yellow – the color of pus. They remained put on the other side of the room.

Kian grabbed Logan with one hand and me with the other, his wings flapping as we made for the window...

Once I had left Delano's side, our strategic position was lost – the guards began rushing towards us.

Kian's wings lifted us off the ground, towards the window, but we were slow...

"We're too heavy," cried Logan!

The guards were coming closer; one of them caught hold of my foot, and I shrieked as I kicked him away.

"Come on."

"Let me go!" cried Logan, as Kian's wings struggled against gravity. We had made it out the window, now, but we could see the archers lining up on the parapets, waiting to let loose their arrows.

A whir of arrows flew past us; one of them struck Logan in the shoulder and he howled.

"Let me go – otherwise we'll all die!"

"It would be dishonorable," cried Kian.

"*Screw* dishonorable!" cried Logan, and bit down upon Kian's wrist as we flew. Kian opened his hand in surprise, and Logan fell – down, down, down until he landed with a nauseating *thud* onto Delano's balcony. I heard the crack of bone, saw the guards rush to him and raise their spears...

I looked away as they brought the blade down.

We flew faster and faster into the night.

It was the bravest thing I had ever seen a man do.

Chapter 13

✳

Kian and I flew into the night; I kept my eyes squeezed shut, unable to stand the tears squeezing through them.

Be strong, I thought to myself.

Be strong, Breena. But it was no use. I could not stop the tears from flowing down beneath us into the night, could not stop my guilt. It was my fault, after all. I had insisted we go back for Kian – and we had – and Logan had died to protect us both: the woman he cared for, and the man he despised. I tried to tell myself that I had no way of knowing what would happen, no way to assess the risks, but it made no difference. I had made my choice – and I had decided who would live and who would die – and I had as good as killed Logan myself.

At last Kian and I descended to a small glen in the middle of a snowy wood. In the glen there was a small manor-house, with a thatched roof, covered with snow. Sharp mistletoe adorned the doorway, and the windows were obscured by pine trees.

"What is this place?" I whispered. My throat was dry and my voice was croaky.

"It is one of the outposts for fairies in this part of the country," said Kian. "There are many – only Winter magic will unlock them – this region is dangerous. It was part of the Safety Policy we initiated at the beginning of the wars – they are for traveling fairies of any sort."

"Is it safe?"

"The strongest magic in Feyland protects us," he said, "It is not far from the Court. I will take you there tomorrow myself, and then the exchange will be made." His voice almost wavered. "You will go home to your family. I will have my family here with me in the Winter Court. I will not trouble you again. You will be able to return home to the mortal world – at least for now."

He tried to maintain his customary regal air; his voice was shaking.

He took my hand at last. "I am sorry for what has befallen you," he said. "I never meant you harm. It was only...."

"An affair of state," I said, bitterly.

He looked miserable. "Your friend was very honorable," he said, "Very brave. Most unlike an ordinary werewolf. He died a hero's death and you should be very proud of him. A man can ask for nothing greater."

"Yeah, how about being alive?" I said, and sniffled.

He put out an arm, giving me an awkward embrace, his back still stiff – the posture of a warrior, of a soldier.

"There is no greater honor than to die in battle for a woman whom one loves," said Kian. "That is the way of the Winter Court."

"Logan didn't..." but my voice trailed off. I knew deep down that I had been lying to myself, and the guilt rose up in my throat again. Logan had always been there. He had always stood by me, supporting me in everything I did, encouraging me to be the best I can be, accepting me for who and what I am. He had come looking for me in Feyland to make sure I was safe, to bring me home. Now he was gone. It was too late. I was going home, but I couldn't bring Logan home safely with me.

I couldn't help it; I started crying at last'– great, racking, heaving sobs that overwhelmed me. It had been a long day – too long a day – and everything was so new, so strange.

"Bree..." Kian said, hugging me close. "Princess."

"It's all my fault!" I cried. "If I hadn't gone back to rescue you – if I'd been a better fighter..."

He kissed me on the forehead. "Nonsense," he said. "You are – you are one of the bravest women I have ever known, Princess, Summer Court or not. You learned the ways of magic and broke your way out of the Pixie Prison. You taught yourself to bring down the chandelier when we were trying to escape. You kept your head when under the threats of the Pixie King. You chose to save me – although you knew the risks – because your sense of honor would not permit you to leave a soldier behind. You came up with a plan– you held a knife to the throat of the Pixie King himself – all within a few days of coming to fairyland! You are a remarkable woman, Breena," he said. "No wonder Logan would risk everything for you."

I was sixteen. I had never thought of myself as a "woman" before. But I had grown older since coming to Feyland. Much older. And now I understood.

I remembered him as I had seen him in my dreams – his beauty, his intensity, the sense of longing I had felt for him for so long before I had ever met him – these feelings all came rushing back to me, dissolving my pride, dissolving my fear, even, though quite, dissolving my pain. Magic was stronger than fairy law, Kian had said, and as he sat beside me I felt the force of magic overwhelm us – its strength overwhelming. More important than affairs of state. More important than fairy contracts. More important than war.

He leaned in, slowly, hesitantly, his lips trembling near mine.

I remembered what Kian had said about my mother – that she had risked her life – that a fairy kiss burned most humans into madness.

It didn't matter. The risk was worth it.

I kissed him, at last – took his face in mine and allowed myself to succumb to the longing that I had been forcing myself to bury since my arrival in Feyland. It was time.

At once, everything changed. I felt like I had when in the midst of the fairy picture, surrounding by the waltz, as I had when in the deepest trances of magic back at the Pixie Court, like I had in the dreams that had haunted me since my youth. But this feeling was greater, stronger, than that. This was an older magic, a deeper magic, the ancient foundation on which all other magic was built– a longing that had allowed him to cross the Crystal River to find me, a longing that had brought me to him…

And he was kissing me back, and suddenly I knew him – knew his thoughts, knew his feelings, knew his fears and his loves and his secrets, all flooding into my brain as if they were my own. I felt his love for me, his fear, his struggle between duty and passion, his desire, his strength, all overwhelming me; there was no space afterward for thought, or logic, or reason. There was only magic.

The Pixies, the minotaurs, the Crystal River and the transfigured hay – they were all parlor tricks, like a rabbit out of a hat.

This was magic.

I was alive.

As we pulled apart, I couldn't help but laugh. "Still here," I said, softly.

"I knew you would be," he said. "You're strong, Bree. Stronger than any fairy." He gave a little laugh too. "I cannot lie to you, Breena. I have known many fairy women – it is expected, when one is a prince. But I have never been kissed – I have never kissed a woman – like that. It has never been like that." He sighed. "You were once my intended, Breena. What has been bound with magic cannot be unbound." He took my hands in his.

"You are my Queen. I cannot deny it. You have always been."

Chapter 14

✳

After he had kissed me, Kian was delirious in his awkwardness. He offered me mermaid tea; he forgot to heat the whistling kettle. He wondered if we should take a walk; he remembered it was nearly three in the morning. He tripped over the table-cloth and confused the butter knife with the jam knife. On his face there was a smile I had never seen before, a picture of true happiness and ebullient joy. I had never seen anyone look happier, more exquisitely radiant in my life!

Until I looked in the mirror. I looked different, I thought – so much older. The kiss had brought rosiness to my cheeks and a sparkle to my eyes I had not seen before. I could not wipe the smile off my face even if I tried.

"It is late," said Kian, after we had finished eating some bread with jam and butter to settle our aching stomachs. "We must go to sleep, and we shall solve everything on the morrow. There is – there is a bedroom upstairs – and here, downstairs, there is the couch." He stumbled over his words. He looked less like a prince, then, less like a restrained and honorable prince of the Royal Court, all cold and noble, and more like a young man, alive and full of energy, of desire.

"Stay," I whispered, and took a corner of the couch, curling up with him. I wanted his strong arms around me in the morning when I woke.

"It is not right," he said. "I will not insult you..."

I smiled. "Don't worry," I said. "I mean – I only mean... stay until I fall asleep."

I fell asleep with his fingers stroking my hair as I dozed into unconsciousness. I could feel him kiss my hair and forehead before he tiptoed upstairs to sleep.

He woke me in the morning with another kiss.

"Good morning, Princess," he said. He took my hand. "You've been sleeping like you've been bitten by the Lethe Bug."

"That probably makes more sense in fairyland," I said, rubbing my eyes. The sun was hot in the air; it must have been afternoon.

Kian's eyes roamed my face lovingly. Without warning, he took me into his arms then and kissed me softly and then deeply. I responded back, winding my hands into his thick black hair and pulling him closer. When we finally broke apart, our breaths were ragged, and we held each other tightly. "Oh Breena," Kian said. "I wish – I wish we can hold each other like this forever. I wish we were not who we are so circumstances between us would be different." He put his face to mine where our cheeks touched each other's. "Ah Breena, my Breena, what has fate done to us?" said Kian, and laughed bitterly. "I – I must apologize for last night. What happened could not be."

"Why?" I sat up.

"As a chivalrous soldier – as a man – I cannot keep the lady I love imprisoned," he said. "But as a Prince of the royal Court, I have a duty to follow the commands of my Queen, to whom I have sworn allegiance and fealty beyond that of any other bond..." he said gravely. "I cannot deny my... inclinations towards you; nor can I deny that there is little I love so well as the Winter Court! I do not want to see it burned up by Summer – and this is a war, Princess. My family, my people, my country is under siege from yours; as long as there is war – to love you would be treasonous."

"Don't worry," I said. "Don't you see – if we unite our kingdoms – if we were to… join together – surely then the war would have to stop!" (Marriage? I thought, in the back of my mind. I was beginning to sound like Kian. I had no desire to get married, for goodness's sake – I was only sixteen, and had had enough of proposals following Delano's attempt on me.)

"It is impossible," said Kian. "Even if we were to defy the wishes of the current rulers – who would never allow it – I promise you – we would have to contend with our duty to our people. The winter fairies trust me; when you ascend to the throne, the summer fairies will trust you! How will it look as a ruler if you succumb to your passions, your feelings, for the *enemy*, no less, instead of leading your people? If the two of us were to marry, we would be forced to unite our kingdoms; how could Summer and Winter fairies live side by side. Two different sets of customs, of traditions! There would be the question of the occupation of the Autumn villages; there would be the question of language, of military forces. Your people would always see you as having betrayed them and put a winter king on the throne – think how many of them know Winter as the land that killed their sons, their husbands, their fathers in war..."

"But we were intended, once!" I cried.

"That was before the war," he said, darkly. "Since then much has changed in Feyland."

He had a point. I had paid attention in history class well enough to know the basics of politics, and I gathered that allowing a hated enemy on your throne wasn't the best or smartest move.

I slipped my hand in his. "We'll figure it out," I said. "Together. We'll find a way to make peace." I had always been a hippie, I thought to myself.

"Easier said than done!" said Kian.

But he took my hand and kissed it. He allowed his eyes to linger over my face, his expression full of adoration, of passion, of love. "My Queen," he said. "My prisoner – my Queen." He stood. "I cannot keep you here," he said. "And yet I must keep you here..." I saw the torment in his eyes, the frustration he had in loving me, yet loving his kingdom. Fate and the law of magic had an ironic sense of humor.

"Stop," I said. "I am not your prisoner any longer. I am a willing delegate from the Summer Court, offering myself up willingly in order to help broker peace in the region. So you can stop worrying about your honor. I'm as free as you are, Kian, and I want to stay with you. I want to help fix this. And," I cupped his cheek in my hand, "I want to give you your sister back."

He smiled through his gloom.

"I will take you to the Winter Court," he said. "But we will find a way. Do not worry, Breena. We will find some way... I – my heart, my soul won't give you up so easily."

Chapter 15

✳

We went through all the possible options in trying to figure out what to do next. We considered first taking me straightaway to the Winter Court and trying to get the whole debacle over with as quickly as possible, but such a tactic gave us a great deal of pause. We feared in the end that the Winter Queen might not hold up her end of the bargain.

"She has been known to torture prisoners," said Kian, with a coolness that terrified me – considering that she was his mother. "And to leave them for days festering in the dungeon. I do not wish to risk your beautiful head on such an agonizing fate."

"Well, let's avoid that, then."

"Sometimes she is perfectly pleasant to them," Kian continued. "It all depends on what mood she is in. And of course how much she misses Shasta."

"Surely she must miss her dreadfully," I said. "After all, Shasta is her child!"

"So am I," said Kian dryly, "and I don't think she thinks much of me. I am an heir – that is all – and I am useful so long as I am fit to govern. If I am found unfit – if the Fairy Court deems me an insufficient ruler – say, if I were to be found liaising with a future Summer Queen – no doubt she would remove me from her sight and lock me away in some cavern up in the northern mountains to prevent my attempting to take over the throne from one of my younger brothers or until I come to my senses."

"But she's your mother!" I cried out. "Surely she must love you."

"I have said," Kian said, "We fairies have tried to limit love long ago. When we have magic such as ours – things that lead to deep magic are far, far too dangerous not to be sanctioned by laws. And love leads to some of the deepest, most uncontrolled magic of all."

"In our world," I said, "Love runs free – we're allowed to marry who we want, and to date who we want for that matter, and we're free to act on our feelings!"

"Yes," said Kian. "And in your world there is a great deal of war – this fairy war is the only one of its kind – and there is selfishness, there is divorce, there are people who let their feelings run away with them and blow up buildings. I know all about your world. You do not sanction love– and it is dangerous! Imagine how much more dangerous it would be if magic were involved. Your world would not survive it."

"We've survived a lot of things," I said hotly. "We're not so bad."

"In any case," continued Kian, "I am perfectly content in the knowledge that she does not love me. She respects me – and that is far more important."

"My mother loves me," I said.

"Your mother was never Queen," said Kian. "Your mother never had to run an empire. She was only a concubine."

I went white with rage. "How dare you?" I said. "My mother was the best – the strongest woman you'd ever know! And if she were here right now, she'd solve this mess with a lot more common sense than any of you so-called rational fairies ever could!"

I stormed into the upstairs bedroom and remained there until sunset. At last I heard a knock at the door.

"Come in!" I said miserably.

Kian entered, stiffly and awkwardly. "It is not the way of fairy princes to apologize," he said. "But I owe you an apology. I meant no ill of your mother – in our world, concubines are not without respect. They fulfill a vital role in fairy society, and the more enlightened among us can respect it. There is certainly no – innuendo – associated with the position. It is seen as lesser than that of Queen, of course, in the same manner that an Emerald Knight is seen as inferior to a Gold Knight, in terms of rank. But I was not – I had no intention – of making you think that your mother was anything but a well-respected woman of the Summer court."

I couldn't help but give a weak laugh. "I guess we've got some culture shock to figure out," I said.

"But I must say," Kian said. "If you are to be offended when I speak of your mother as a concubine – I must ask that you understand if I prefer you not to act as if there is something unspeak-able in my lacking my mother's love. That is the way of things here, as other things are the way of things in your land. And you are a Halfling, after all; you must learn to adopt both ways. If you are to rule the Summer Court, after all, you must learn fairy custom."

"I'm sorry too," I said. "It's just hard for me – getting used to all this. It's all so new – and every time I turn around there's some custom that just seems crazy to me. Where I come from, love is... well, you listen to the radio and every single song is about love. And here, it's frowned upon! Viewed as a sign of weakness! Everything's so... technical here."

"I find your world very perplexing," said Kian. "For one thing, your idea of entertainment – a film, they call it? It's only in two dimensions, and you can't even control the players!"

I realized that beneath his gruff exterior he was trying to make a joke. I laughed.

"We'll manage," I said to him. "Don't worry."

He smiled at me. "We will never make peace between the Winter and Summer Courts if we cannot first broker peace between fairies and humans," he said. "Come, let us sign a treaty of our own."

He took me downstairs, to where a sumptuous banquet awaited us.

"I thought you would be more prone to forgive me if I prepared dinner," said Kian.

The delicious smell of roasting vegetables and potatoes wafted into my nostrils.

"It is a traditional fairy meal," said Kian. "In Feyland, it is traditionally men that do the cooking. It is seen as a symbolic presentation of the hunt."

I decided there were some customs I preferred in Feyland after all.

After dinner we decided that Kian and I would hide out in the manor until we could better assess the situation and tell whether or not the Winter Queen would be amenable to the Geneva Conventions.

If there were many more meals like that ahead of me, waiting would certainly not be so hard.

Chapter 16

✳

Kian and I decided together that we should make the most of the time we had together, as we lay low and Kian tried to get a sense of the goings-on of the Fairy Courts. He had sent a letter, the paper curled round the foot of a dove, to one of his closest friends at the fairy court, asking him what the circumstances were in the land of Winter and how the Winter Queen planned to treat the Princess Breena when she found her.

The letter, we knew, would take some days to arrive, and in the meanwhile I asked Kian to teach me more about the ways of Feyland.

"If I have to fight off a pixie," I said, "I want to make sure I'm doing it properly."

"That display with the chandelier was quite impressive," said Kian. "Certainly a good start."

"That was dumb luck," I said.

"Well," said Kian. "I think the first place we should start is discussing the source of your magic. Every fairy has one. An image, a thought, a piece of music, a sound that allows you to harness to power within you. When you performed that stunning piece of teleportation, what were you thinking of?"

I remembered my concentration on Kian's face, the feeling of love and longing I experienced when I let the sound of the fairy waltz overtake me, and against myself I blushed.

"I wasn't thinking of anything," I said. "Just how to get out alive – I just wanted to live, that's all."

"That can't be," said Kian. "Magic doesn't work that way. You'll have to tap into it somehow."

"You'll laugh," I said. "I know you will!"

"I won't laugh at you," Kian promised. "You have my word."

"Well," I began, "when I was little – in fact, my whole life, even up to my sixteenth birthday in the mortal world, I always had... how can I put it? This dream. This dream about the Summer Court. And you and I were children, then, and laughing and dancing – we were learning the fairy waltz, which in my dream – and I know this is stupid, Kian, – was going to play at our wedding."

He had gone pale.

"And whenever I try to tap into the magic, I just think of that fairy waltz – and you, I guess," I added hurriedly, trying to swallow my words. My face had gone beet-red. "And somehow I'm able to perform whatever magic I need to perform. Maybe because you taught me how magic worked – I don't know. I wouldn't read anything into it; it's just silly."

He grabbed hold of my hand.

"I have had that dream many a time, Breena," said Kian. "Often I would refuse to let myself sleep while preparing for battle, for I knew that the dream would come and distract me from my purposes. I remember the waltz better than you might think."

He began to hum it – the song I knew, the song that we had shared – his voice beautiful and melodic, echoing through the stone walls of the manor.

"It's gorgeous..." I breathed.

"Yes," he said. "It is a wedding song. It is our song, Breena, only yours and mine. Every fairy marriage has a song – it is created by the union of the two intended fairies. And that song is ours – created out of our souls." He pressed his lips to my fingers, then got up abruptly, embarrassed. "It is good," he said, "that you have such a strong source of your magic. It is dangerous – I have told you that love-magic often is – but nevertheless it is very much a strength, if you can use it correctly."

"What's your source?" I asked.

Kian colored and looked away.

"We should get down to lessons."

The first thing Kian taught me was how to use a sword. "It is heavy," he warned me, "I only have men's swords here. Women's swords are lighter and more agile. We have female warrior-knights among the winter court, but there are none at the moment."

I felt the weighty metal in my hand.

"I was never very good at P.E.," I laughed grimly as I traced my fingers down the sharp blade. "So, do I have to start working out?"

"You have two choices," he said. "You can wield your sword as men of your world do" – using your body, moving the sword with your hands. Or you can use magic. Both are worthy – there are times when mortal men, or fairies fighting in the mortal manner, have overcome fairy ways by the surprising use of a good mortal feint or parry. But I suggest you start with the magical ways; a woman of your size might have difficulty going up against a pixie with nothing but her strength to sustain her. I suggest you ultimately learn both ways, however; as a Halfling, you ought to make use of both your halves of talent."

I closed my eyes and seized the handle of the sword, willing it to move and shake and protect me.

"Forge a bond with the sword," said Kian. "It must *want* to protect you. If it dislikes you, you may find yourself tripped and fallen upon it."

"Sounds dangerous," I said, eying my sword warily.

"Magic is dangerous," said Kian, and shrugged. "Go on now, try and fight me."

I couldn't will the sword to attack Kian if I tried. It stood limp in my hands.

"That's not fair," I said. "How am I supposed to try to hurt you?"

"You won't hurt me," he said, holding up his sword. "No disrespect, my Princess, but I have been training as a soldier for many fairy-years. Think of it as a challenge. Whoever loses the battle will have to cook dinner tonight!"

I thought of the sumptuous feast Kian had prepared for me the night before and my mouth watered. And then an image, however fleeting, of Logan preparing tortillas on my kitchen counter flashed into my mind – as carefree and happy as he had always been, in the days that we had been so close, so intimate! How could I have almost forgotten him already? Tears stung my eyes, as I remembered his death, that final climactic battle. If I had been able to fight, then, then perhaps Logan would still be alive, still be here...

The sword leaped in my hand, powerful and red-hot, soaring towards Kian's shield.

It knocked the sword out of his hand with a loud clatter; he stared at me, shocked. He had not been expecting me to strike so well; he had not bothered to be on his guard.

"All that for a nice dinner?" he said, with a faint smile.

The tears remained in my eyes.

"Logan..." I whispered.

His face clouded. For a moment he almost looked angry. Certainly there a hint of jealousy that swept across his regal face. Then he came up to me and gathered me into his arms, whispering my name over and over into my hair.

"He died a hero," said Kian, because that was the only comforting thing he knew to say.

"But he *died*," I hissed.

My commitment to learning self-defense increased tenfold. We learned swordplay and archery, the riding of horses (I remembered clinging to Logan's back when he was in wolf-form and this too brought tears to my eyes), magical dueling, and other pursuits, breaking up the physical exertions with discussions of Fey History and the lore of Feyland. Kian had brought out his old academic textbooks from the days when he had been tutored by one of the ancient professors of his race.

"I never much liked them," he said, but nevertheless I devoured them – the dull genealogies and talk of fairy politics as much as the exciting stories of mythical creatures that far outstripped anything in *Causabon's Mythology*..

And every night, I would fall asleep in Kian's arms and wake up to his morning kiss. He would hold my face in his hands, gently as though he would never want our moments together to end.

By necessity we muted our romance, subsuming it into days of fencing and riding and study, knowing that we had no time for anything more than a chaste, stolen kiss between bouts of lessons. But when I slept I felt the warmth of his arms around me, and I wished, in some deep part of myself, that the answer to his letter could be delayed just a little longer.

Chapter 17

✳

Time moved slowly in those days – slowly but beautifully. Kian and I spent sunrise to sunset together, helping me become the best fairy queen that I could be. The things we learned together were of the sort that even my most frenzied dreams back home in Gregory, Oregon, could never have guessed at. I learned how to fight, of course, to guide my sword or dagger or even bow and arrow into the heart of an enemy foe. I learned to vanish into invisibility, only to reappear moments later around some hidden corner. I learned to treat the air itself as if it were earth, treading on clouds and fog and even clear breezes, running and jumping in the air. I learned, too, some special powers – ways in which I even outranked Kian. As a Summer Princess, I found that I had a special affinity for the sun; when I concentrated, I found myself able to lock into the power of the great golden orb itself – to radiate energy, becoming like a sun myself, glowing with power and magic. These powers coursed through me; once I learned them, it seemed that I had always known them, that they had always been part of me – I just hadn't realized it yet.

Kian, for his part, was extraordinarily proud of me; his pale arctic nose went faintly pink with pleasure whenever I found myself able to outmatch him in a game of magical wits – to run faster, to prove myself stronger. He was, of course, far more experienced than I was, but I took great pleasure in even the tiniest victory over him, and in time I came to score increasingly more points, until Kian dispensed with handicaps and "beginner's luck" altogether and began seriously exerting himself in order to keep the lead he had held so easily in the first days of my magical training.

I cannot tell how long we stayed in the manor; it seemed, in those wonderful days, like an eternity. Time stood in place or else glided slowly – like a woman dancing to a soft waltz – and nothing seemed real outside of the world of fairy magic that we too had created. Even the pain of Logan's death – like a knot in my chest – loosened after a while; as I worked in the realm of magic, I began to feel that rather Logan – wherever he was – was somehow part of that ancient set of rituals, that his love and nobility were not lost with his destruction at the hands of the Pixie King Delano, but rather absorbed somehow into the great and wonderful world about which I was learning so much.

One morning I decided to put my training into practice and go hunting for deer for that day's lunch – a surprise for Kian, and one that I felt sure would solidify my status as his equal in magic. He had taught me to distinguish between those deer that were for eating and those that were to be left as magical equals, to engage with the deer I hunted and participate in the magic that allowed the arrow to pierce the deer, the deer to willingly give up its life as part of the circle of birth and death and renewal. I felt sure that deer would be meager compared to the rare options Kian was able to bring down and cook with such skill, but nevertheless I wanted to do something to contribute to the little life we were building together in the manor.

I sat crouched and hidden within the woods, waiting for a herd of deer to pass me by. The sun was bright and golden in the sky; the air was cool and crisp and delicious. I could feel the warm heat of afternoon prickling comfortably at my back. It was a perfect day.

Before long I caught sight of a running herd of deer, whirring with graceful agility through the forest. I concentrated, biting my lower lip as I did so, and aimed my arrow straight towards one of the blurry brown shapes passing by me.

I tensed my arm against the bow, remembering my physical training as well as my magical one, and let the arrow fly.

And then I felt the arrow pierce my calf.

I winced, confused despite the searing pain. I had shot away from me... what happened?

I heard another sound, the whirring of an arrow through the air, and narrowly dodged it.

Danger.

I looked around me. There, in the distance, was a cavalcade of knights on horseback, each more beautiful, more splendid than the next. They carried golden bows with them – but did not even so much as buckle under the weight of the gem-encrusting things. They seemed to radiate golden brightness as they rode towards me, noble and upright on their galloping steeds. I knew them by the armor they wore – the orange-and-golden metal – but I would have recognized them even if they were wearing human clothes, so bright and strong was their demeanor. They were my knights– knights of the summer court.

Thinking the arrow in my calf must have been an accident, a stray from the hunt, I looked up, focusing my magic on silencing the pain coming from my leg. These were my men – perhaps here to rescue me! I would explain; everything would be fixed in the end.

And then two of the men grabbed hold of my arm and twisted it around, hard.

"What are you doing?" I asked.

"You're under arrest," barked one of the men. They began tying my hands behind my back with fairy chains; the gold dug into my flesh.

"I am Princess Breena of the Fairy Court," I said, in my best imperial voice. "Release me at once! I have been waiting for the Summer Court to come find me."

"We know exactly who you are," said the other man, and my heart sank.

"What are you doing? Can't you see I'm a princess?" I almost shouted at him.

"Afraid we're just following orders, Highness," said one of the knights. "We answer to the Summer Queen, and she's put out a warrant for your arrest."

"For what?" I asked, suddenly wondering if what Kian and I had been doing would get me into trouble at the home court. "I haven't done anything wrong; I've been kidnapped."

"You've entered the fairy realm after being banished," said the knight. "The whole point of exile is that you stay over the Crystal River; the second you came back over, you breached fairy law."

"What?" This was new to me, and confusing. "But I didn't come here, anyway; I was kidnapped..."

I stopped speaking immediately, realizing my mistake. The last thing I wanted to do was have Kian woken up by some vicious fairy knights with a price on his head, too.

"Take it up with the Queen at the fairy castle," said the guard. "You'll have plenty of chances to speak your case at the trial," he said, with a smirking laugh that gave me some lingering doubts about the fairness and efficacy of the fairy judicial system.

And with that they thrust me onto their horses and began spiriting me away.

I tried to call out to Kian, using my magic, trying to open a doorway between our two minds.

I focused on his face with all my energy, squeezing my eyes shut.

Kian, I called out, *Kian.*

And then I gasped. For a moment I felt as if I were inside Kian's head, feeling what he felt, experiencing what he experienced. And Kian was waking up to find a series of fairy daggers pointed at his throat. These were cold, frightening creatures – Winter Knights – his own men! Flynn, with a scowl, was at the head of them.

"We are under orders to return you to the Winter Court immediately," said Flynn, pressing the dagger into Kian's throat; I could feel its point on my own.

I could feel Kian reach for his sword; the dagger pressed in more deeply.

"We have orders to kill you if you resist," said Flynn. "The Winter Queen is most displeased with your actions."

"Bree..." I could hear him call, and my heart called out to him in response.

"Yes, the girl," said Flynn. "We no longer need her alive."

I could feel the pain in Kian's chest as my fairy knights sped me away. He was far more worried about me than his own welfare. "Breena!" he cried out loud again, his eyes flying around the room, frantically looking for me.

"All your calling won't bring her back," Flynn said.

Kian's eyes opened wide, and his face colored with fury. "If you so much..." he began, stopping himself. He bunched up his hands into fists. I can feel his anguish, his fear for me, his sadness if the worse had happened to me.

Flynn's eyebrows arched slightly. "So has it come to this? Has our revered crowned Winter Prince been succumbing to his feelings over the Queen's prisoner? The knights all know how she was once your intended. Why that would be trea..."

Kian looked down. All the feelings, all the love he had for me stirred him to the core when he thought of any harm that could have befallen me.

Finally, he looked up, steeling himself, composing his mind, his heart. "She is but the Winter Queen's prisoner," he said. "I risked life and limb to find her and bring her to the Queen. Do not be stupid, Flynn. Do you think I would betray my sister so readily? Where is Breena?"

Flynn was taken aback as though he was confused by Kian's response. "She cannot be found here," he said. "We have a far better prisoner in her stead. As far as the Fairy Court is concerned, she's fair game for bounty hunters now."

I could feel the shock and surprise in Kian's mind. I can feel his regret that he cannot truly confess his love for me, that he had to hide it, suppress it, refrain from letting it rule his logic, like he had tried to suppress the same dream I have always had about Kian and I at the Summer Court, dancing our fairy waltz, our souls and fate entwined.

I closed my eyes, willing the tears not to come, and amid my tears I felt a terrible confusion. Who could this other prisoner be? And what would happen to all of us?

Chapter 18

✳

The guards escorted me into the Summer Palace. It was nothing like I remembered. The parapets and turrets had once been my hiding-places; I remembered, out of the corners of my mind, the soft, melting gold of the steps and the banisters, the gorgeous tapestries rich and warm on the white stone. Now, the palace was still warm – it was the Summer Palace, after all – but its warmth was like a white-hot flame, or a burning ember – remote, mysterious, and ultimately frightening. It was not a warmth I liked; instead, I felt myself growing hot as I entered, as if I had walked inadvertently into a furnace; my face flushed and grew red, and I began to stagger. I held my head up as high as I could, focusing with all my strength on the task that lay ahead of us. I had to figure out what was going on, to see the Summer Queen eye to eye, and to try and understand what it was I had done, in the bright days of my infancy that could have possibly gotten me banished from the Court. Me – a Princess!

Life was strange here in the fairy kingdom, I thought. A Princess could be banished from her own court; a Queen could threaten her own son, a fairy Prince, with death! It had been so beautiful in my dreams, this place, but since my return I could not help but feel that the dangers of the cities and the forests were too new, too terrifying. It was not the fairyland I remembered from my dreams. It was a darker place.

The guards escorted me inside and I saw her sitting on a throne made of golden columns, with rubies inlaid down and around the building. I had dreamed many times of the Summer Court, but I had never dreamed of her in any of those nights. Nevertheless, I recognized her; my magic found and responded to hers. How could it not? Her magic was overwhelming. Her hair was long and so golden that it was almost white, her tresses falling into her lap and down the sides of her seat, tangling in one another. Her eyes were a warm brown – like the color of cinnamon – flecked with gold, eyes I could see were fixing on me with predatory interest as I entered. She wore a long, flowing dress of crushed red velvet; it only accentuated her deep, glowing skin. She was beautiful; she was also terrible. She was the Summer Queen.

She was a venerable ruler; from the moment I entered I knew that it was she who ran the Summer Court; she exuded power from the hem of her heavy skirt to the crown she wore perched upon her head.

"So," she said. "Here at last, are we?" She smiled and it was not a smile of friendship. "Do you remember me at all, Breena?"

I shook my head, still awe-struck by the power of this fiery figure.

She laughed, and her laughter echoed through the palace halls. "And to think," she said, "there was a time when you used to run in here, covered in fairy-flowers and water from one of the fountains in the gardens, run and embrace me. Do you remember what you used to call me, Breena?"

I shook my head again.

"Mother Queen, you called me. Mother Queen."
She put the matter aside. "And now you don't remember me at all! I'm not surprised, the way your
mother brought you up. Of course, one must make
allowances for concubines."

I reddened.

"Please, Your Highness," I began, my voice
shaking as I felt that "Mother Queen" would have
the opposite of the desired effect. "Where is..." I
meant to ask for the king; the words reshaped
themselves in my mouth. "...my father?"

She scoffed.

"Out beyond the Crystal River somewhere," she
said mockingly, her voice full of scorn. "In your
realm. Cavorting with one or the other of the maids
from that side of the universe – he's got such a
weakness for mortal women! It really is sickening!"

"He's in the mortal world?" I repeated. "Why?"

"I don't care who she is," said the Summer
Queen, "as long as her name isn't Raine – that's all
that matters to me. He can have his fun – but he'd
sacrifice the whole Summer Court to that woman!
And I can't have that happening."

"He's with another woman?" I asked.

"While I'm left to run a country and fight a war by myself." She smiled. "All by myself – can you believe it? You see what I have to put up with!"

I could not help feeling a little sorry for her. I had seen what the fairy war had done to Feyland; I would not have wanted her position for the world.

"Typical men," she said, and then remembered that I was there. "Well then, Breena," she continued, "You've put us all in quite a state. You always were a trouble-maker. I remember how dirty you used to get – you used to run and play hide-and-seek and the servants would have a time of it trying to catch you."

I thought of my father in Feyland. I couldn't believe what the Summer Queen was saying – that he was there in the mortal world only to lay his eyes on mortal women. No, he was my father, after all, even if I didn't know him. He had to have been looking for my mother, trying desperately to warn us of the danger...

"You're getting to be quite a nice-looking young lady, I must admit," she said. "Although it pains me to do so. Rather like your mother when she was young." She sighed, heavily. "She was only a little older than you were when she met my husband. And how he fell for her! I've never seen any-thing like it! The other ones he would hide away, he would be discreet about. But not her! He in-sisted that she had to be near him at all times, that he had to put her up at Court, you see, at my Court, and that her children would inherit...ah, well, but that's my curse, you see, as well as the curse of so many powerful fairies. We are all bar-ren, barren as the trees of the Winter Court. And so our court has to make do with Halflings like you."

"That isn't to say I didn't enjoy the sound of children playing in the Court – while it lasted. You and the Winter children all running about rambunctiously while your father played with you like the child he was! But it didn't matter, then. There was no war, then, not until we were at-tacked..."

"Attacked?" I asked.

"The Winter Court," she said, "set a trap for us. The traitors." Her mouth and eyes contorted in disgust. "But I blame you. You, child, have been a problem for us since the day you were born – you and your mother, with your magic, attracting trouble everywhere you went! I knew you had strong magic – from the time you were a child. I saw a kewpie try to come into your crib once; at six months of age you were able to repel it. And usually it takes two grown men to do that! Danger will follow you wherever you go, you and your kind. At last I made your father see sense. He didn't want to, of course, but at last I persuaded him to banish the both of you for the good of this whole kingdom."

My father had agreed to send me away? My eyes welled with tears. How could I be dangerous? What had I done? I was only a baby then!

Life in the fairy court was getting stranger and stranger.

Chapter 19

✳

When the Summer Queen had finished speaking, she was interrupted by the arrival of a messenger. He was a slim, golden creature – a small fairy page-boy with eyes like the summer sun, wearing a long scarlet tunic. I tried to use the time he spent whispering in her ear to gather my thoughts. I was nervous, of course – absolutely terrified! – but beyond that I was worried about myself. What could I have done, I thought? What had I done that was so wrong, so wicked, so dangerous that my own father would send me away beyond the Crystal River – and my mother, too? I, the fairy Queen had said, had trouble everywhere I went – it dogged my footsteps. Was she right? I thought of the Pixie King, of Kian, of Logan (and a lump rose in my throat when I thought of Logan) and at once I wasn't sure whether I could deny it.

The Queen looked up as the pageboy left. Her demeanor was expressionless, the marble countenance of a great Queen bearing secrets of state. – "Well," she said. "It seems that we will soon have a visitor here in the Summer Court, Breena. What think you of that?"

"I – I don't know, Your Highness," I stammered.

She smiled a grim smile. "The Winter Court has sent us a letter."

"What does it say?" I asked, too-eager, thinking of Kian.

"Well," she said, "Let me tell you what it says. It offers me a very interesting deal. And I'm curious – Princess – should I take it?"

"What is it?"

"An exchange of prisoners," she said. "Interesting indeed. The Winter Court has someone very intriguing they would like to offer me in exchange for the Princess languishing down there in the dungeons. They do say that it would be a peaceful exchange..."

I thought of Kian, of our nights and days together at the manor, and wished he were here alongside me, to talk of peace, of hope. We had promised each other that we would find some way, some how, to make peace between the two kingdoms; having seen the harsh ferocity of the Summer Court, my hopeful heart was slowly sinking. How silly must I have been to think that I – a mere girl of sixteen – could fight battles of centuries of fairy history. I swallowed hard.

"Who are the prisoners?" I asked.

"Funny you should ask," said the Summer Queen. "Let's see." Her voice was like clotted honey; it stuck in her throat. "Your opinion on this matter will indubitably be most, most entertaining. You see, the prisoner that the Winter Court wants is its oldest daughter, Shasta. Perhaps you remember her! You played with each other when the two of you were children, and we were not yet at war with the Winter Court."

"And the other prisoner?" I said warily. I had once been the other prisoner; who else could it be?

The Summer Queen's lips closed in a smirk. "Your mother," she said.

I gasped. My mother! I thought of her mysteriously vanished on the morning of my birthday – it seemed so long ago! – and my throat tightened.

What would they do with her? She was my mother – my protectress – the idea that anything could have happened to her was still unthinkable to me.

"Now, I don't care a fig about your mother. She's nothing but a dangerous concubine – the Winter Court can have her for all I care! But there is one problem." She peered at me. "Your silly father. As long as the favorite concubine of the Summer King is in the Winter Court, they have a huge hold of us – for you know he would fight a hundred thousand pixies to get to her, let alone some Winter fairies. And if the Winter Court has – *him*, well... I have been ruling this court for years – but ruling without even the appearance of a king by my side! But the Summer fairies love their king and would not stand for any Summer royalty to be a prisoner of the Winter Court. They come in peace, they say, but I don't trust them. We trusted them years ago when we allowed the Winter Court to visit us, only to be betrayed and tricked, attacked right in our own palace. That was what started this war."

"Now, Breena," she continued. "You think you have the right to take my place one day, don't you? Of course you do. You see, being a queen takes more cunning and wisdom, more strength to do the right thing for your people, and more fortitude than you would think. A queen should be the equal match of a king (in my case, even stronger) because of the enormous fate a queen controls for many. And a queen should be willing to sacrifice her life and dreams for her kingdom. So why don't you give me the answer to this... conundrum? What would you do? Now be careful! I'm still Queen, and if I don't like your answer, I can always send you to the Pitchkey Dungeons. You'll be rat food there – if you're lucky."

I stood limply before her, my mind cycling through centuries of fairy history, fairy learning, trying desperately to think what to do....

Epilogue

�֍

A dream, feverish and terrifying, coming over me again and again.

A dungeon, dank and moldy, with stone walls and the scurrying of rats around the hay. A terrible smell – plague, pus, agony. No light except for the torches on the walls, the gleam in the guards' eyes. Pixie guards. Some of them recognizable – these are Delano's men. Cold. Ugly. Evil.

A figure, lying in the middle of the floor, great and hulking, covered in so much blood I cannot see the fur or figure underneath. A howl of terror. A scream of pain. Over and over again until I think I am going to wake up in a sweat.

The slow trail of starvation. Terror.

A pixie's voice. – "You know, I think we'd be doing him a favor by ending it."

A low moan from the figure.

"There's only so much torture one of their kind can take. Eventually they go insane, and then you lose all the fun."

A voice, high-pitched and eerie. This is Delano's voice; I recognize it by its cruelty.

"Oh, no," says Delano. "Not at all. We can't kill him. Besides, when Princess Breena hears that her werewolf is still alive – which she will, then nothing will stop her from coming back here to fetch him.

"And then nothing will stop me."

❖ ❖ ❖ ❖ ❖ ❖ ❖ ❖

Breena, Kian, and Logan's story continues in
Book 2 of Bitter Frost

Forever Frost
September 2010

Excerpt from

Rise of the Fire Tamer

The Wordwick Games™

Book 1

kailin gow

Prologue

The deadline slipped past, as deadlines tend to. Around the world, hungry eyes pinned themselves to computer screens, waiting for news. When it came, it came in the form of a simple video file, which when opened showed the familiar head and shoulders of Henry Word, the owner of Wordwick Inc. As heads went, it wasn't too bad. Although he had hit forty, there weren't any signs of gray in the sandy-blond hair, and the cleft chin was still as defined as ever. In the second or two before he started speaking, there was a twinkle in the green eyes that said that Henry Word was enjoying the suspense.

"Well," he began, "you're probably all waiting with baited breath for me to announce the winners of the Wordwick Games Contest, designed to find our ultimate fans. After all, you probably want to know who's getting the prize of spending a week in the castle you all know and love from the game." A mischievous smile flickered across his features for a moment. "Well, simply telling you would hardly be much fun, would it? Instead, I think I'll keep you all in suspense just a little while longer, and our winners..." Henry Word raised a remarkably old-fashioned pocket watch to eye level and spun it like a carnival hypnotist. "Well, our winners should be finding out very soon indeed."

Tumbleweed didn't twist its way across the ranch, because that would have been too much like something happening. Stieg Sparks had learned many things in the past seventeen years, and one of them was that nothing much ever seemed to happen on days when you really wanted them to. Particularly not on his parents' ranch. A few cattle, though not as many as there once had been, stood and stared at Sparks as he sat on the front porch, and he stared back, more for something to do than from any particular interest in them.

The cows were probably getting the better end of the deal, since underneath his sandy-blond hair Sparks had the casual good looks that came with being his school football team's star quarterback, while cows were just cows.

Of course, Sparks knew could probably find something to do, if he set his mind to it. He could do most things once he set his mind to them. He could, for example, go and take a look at the broken crop sprayer that his father had sworn would never work again, before they ended up paying out more money the ranch didn't have. He would probably find a way to get it working. Or he could go inside and log on to the Game, though his mother had started to say he was spending too much time on it.

He could even hurry over to football practice. It was certainly what he was supposed to be doing. He might even make it in time not to earn any extra laps from the coach, if he really rushed. Somehow, the thought didn't spur him to action. In fact, put like that, even staring at cows seemed better.

It occurred to him that they weren't staring back at him any more. Instead, they were busy watching a figure that had somehow managed to walk halfway up the drive to the house without Sparks noticing. Sparks couldn't blame them. The figure wore what could only be described as a robe, the cowl up and obscuring their face. Sparks was so surprised by the arrival that he didn't say anything until the figure was just a couple of feet away.

"Hi. Are you lost?"

In answer, the hooded figure held out a hand. It took Sparks a moment to notice that there was an envelope in it. Sparks took it without thinking. It was an odd sort of envelope, jet-black and sealed in a very old-fashioned way, with a blob of red wax that had a seal pressed into it. The seal formed a capital W. A very familiar capital W, since Sparks had seen it online practically every day for months now.

He ripped it open and read the contents in one go, then looked up to ask the hooded figure about it. Sparks found himself staring at empty space. Well, not exactly empty. There were still the cows. There were always cows. There just seemed to be a complete lack of any gray robed figures to go with them.

THIS apartment was a lot smaller than any ranch, and there certainly wasn't room for any cows, except possibly in the refrigerator. There was hardly space for Rio, his little brother and his grandmother. Sometimes, especially when his grandmother started saying things like "Riordan Roberts! What trouble have you got yourself into this time?" he thought that there might not even be enough room for all three of them.

Or at least not for him. The dark hair and olive skin he'd inherited from his mother were fine with his grandmother, but the piercing blue eyes he'd got from his father weren't so ok. Not after what happened. It didn't strike Rio as very fair that she'd bring it up whenever there was trouble, especially when it was never Rio's fault. Well, not most of the time, anyway. It certainly wasn't down to him that practically everything in East LA seemed to be trouble in Nana's opinion. As far as Rio could see, taking a few things for Nana and Tomas shouldn't really count. He was only looking out for them.

Currently, he was sitting in front of about the only luxury the apartment had, a tiny computer that Nana had insisted the two of them should have for their schoolwork. For once, Rio was using it for just that, and not the Game. He looked up at the sound of soft footfalls behind him, expecting to see Tomas. It wasn't.

"Hey, who are you?"

The figure in gray didn't say anything, and Rio lunged forward to try and wrench the hood of the robe back. If someone was going to break in, he wanted to see their face. He got a brief glimpse of a face almost completely hidden by wraparound sunglasses, before the robe pulled out of his hands, leaving Rio trying to keep his balance and failing. He looked up from the carpet, and the figure was gone. All that was left was a black envelope left precisely on the floor in front of him like the figure had known where he would fall.

It occurred to Rio that, in Grams' book, this would *definitely* count as trouble.

Somewhere in the blare of music that was her bedroom, Kat was taking a lot of trouble over her appearance. Her hair was already right, or at least it was a chin length bob of dark hair with streaks of blue and red that her parents tried very carefully not to disapprove of, but the rest of it hadn't been easy. There had been the red and black plaid to pick out to go with her combat boots, along with exactly the right amount of black makeup. It had taken ages to get right. The makeup aged her a year older than her sixteen years, but didn't help fill out her slim figure. She had even cut short her session on the Game to work on it more.

Let's see Them think I'm ordinary now, Kat thought. She always thought of her parents as Them, especially when they insisted on calling her Katherine instead of Kat, which they did a lot. They seemed to have evolved a policy of ignoring the more extreme things Kat did, in the hopes that eventually she would fit in, or that she would become the Katherine Kipling they wanted her to be. Well fat chance.

Kat surveyed the results of her efforts in her bedroom mirror. Despite her Dark Girl outfit, she still looked like a pixie or what people think pixies should look like, the child-like Tinker Bell version. An independent observer might have suspected that black eye shadow, and black nail polish, *and* black lipstick was probably overdoing things a bit, or was at least a look better suited to someone tall and brooding, not petite and, frankly, cute. Kat loved it.

She was so busy admiring it that she almost didn't notice the reflection of the gray cloaked figure – the one who laid an envelope on the edge of the dressing table but vanished the moment she looked round. It could almost have been a dream, except that the envelope was there, sitting rather smugly, Kat thought, as though it knew exactly how worrying its sudden appearance was.

Still, Kat recovered enough to think after a moment, at least the black went with her nail polish.

Up in Jackson Zusak's home in Alaska, things were a little brighter, mostly because his parents insisted on filling the place with the color that the cold tended to leach away outside. Some days, he could hardly get to his computer for the brightly colored throws and coverings that his mom kept leaving around the place.

He wasn't at his computer now, for once. Instead, he was sitting in an armchair busy reading a book on the history of the Vikings. That had amused his mom and dad when they had seen it before heading off to the store to buy groceries.

"You could be a Viking yourself," Jack's mom had said. "You've got the red hair."

They had all laughed at that, because even Jack knew that the image of his small, scrawny figure setting sail across vast oceans just didn't work. Besides, they didn't have glasses back then, and a Viking who wandered into things, as Jack tended to do when he lost his, probably wouldn't do very well.

"You're only fifteen," his mom had said, hugging him. "You've still got time to grow to be Viking-sized."

Jack hadn't pointed out that, because people tended to be shorter in the past, he was probably already Viking-sized, for much the same reason that he didn't tell his dad the answers to the crossword before he'd officially given up on it. Thinking of which...

Jack found the newspaper in its usual crumpled up heap, smoothed it out a little, and finished off the crossword in a couple of minutes before returning to his book. He'd forgotten to mark his place, and it had closed on the arm of the chair he'd been sitting in. He went to open it again, and almost dropped it when the black envelope fell out. Out of the window, Jack got a brief glimpse of a gray robed figure, hurrying away too quickly to catch.

GEMMA James caught the sound of the doorbell just as she was finishing an assignment for her private school. She was pretty sure she'd aced it. She thought about ignoring the disturbance to go through it once more, but then remembered that there wasn't anyone else home in her family's Manhattan house. It might be a delivery, and since her dad was a lawyer, there was every chance that it might be something important that she would need to sign for, assuming that they'd take a sixteen-year-old's signature.

Sighing, Gem stood up and made her way through the place's expensive furnishings, pausing automatically to check her appearance in the hall mirror. It was one of those habits she had picked up from cheerleading, because you never knew when the universe might have found ways to make you look a mess. As usual, she looked perfect, not a hair of her long blonde hair out of place as it framed a face with porcelain skin and deep green eyes. She smoothed out her skirt, then checked the door's spy hole, because appearance wasn't the only time you couldn't be too careful.

There wasn't anyone there. Or rather, there wasn't anyone standing at the door. There was someone walking away, dressed in the sort of robe that didn't make sense unless Franciscan monks had started making deliveries, but he was gone in a second or two. Gem waited a moment longer before opening the door. She looked around, and found no one there, so she looked down. When she saw the envelope, she smiled very slowly, because some moments deserved to be drawn out, then she picked it up, ripped it open and read it so quickly that it probably set some sort of record.

Chapter 1

As the car that had been sent to the airport crunched its way up the estate's gravel drive and rattled over the drawbridge, Gem found herself quietly surprised. Even though the invitation had said that she and her fellow winners would be staying in the castle at the heart of the Wordwick game, and even though her father, who'd been there on business, had confirmed that it was very much a real castle, she hadn't really believed it. She'd gone online and looked into English castles, only to find that most of the really big ones were publicly owned, or had been ruined in the various wars since the Middle Ages, or both.

She'd expected that the "castle" would just be a manor house with a few battlements tacked on, so her first sight of Henry Word's home left her open mouthed. It was everything its online presence promised; a huge, sprawling circle of stone walls almost totally ringed by a moat and themselves surrounding a square bailey keep at one end, along with outbuildings, gardens, and what looked very much like a maze. From above it would probably have looked like a lopsided archery target.

Parts of the castle had obviously been updated, such as the ground floor entrance to the keep that the car pulled up to, but mostly it looked like it had stayed untouched for hundreds of years. Except that if it really hadn't been touched, then the stonework would be crumbling and the whole place would have been overrun with plant life. Someone had obviously put a lot of effort into looking after it.

Gem got out of the car wondering how Henry Word had managed to get his hands on the place. She knew he was rich – her father had done enough work for him that she had a pretty good idea of just how rich – but even so, it seemed hard to credit. Places like this weren't in private hands, were they? Maybe he still let visitors in. The ramp for wheelchair access to the front door was the sort of thing that they always had for visitors, wasn't it?

The driver handed Gem her bag and wished her a pleasant stay, but she wasn't really listening. She was too busy staring as she stepped through the doors and into the keep's lobby. Her private school was quite old-fashioned in its tastes, full of wood paneled walls and old paintings, but this had it beaten easily. There were expensive looking rugs thrown over the flagstone floor, and tapestries on the walls that blazed with color. They were interspersed with painted shields, and displays of swords or fragments of armor that looked like they really were hundreds of years old. Great oak doors branched off from it through small stone arches. It looked like the sort of thing that might result if someone had told a set designer to make everything look as medieval as possible, and then given them the contents of a museum strong room to use for decoration.

Gem was so busy taking it all in that for almost half a minute she didn't notice the four other people standing in the hallway, and she started when she noticed them. All four seemed to be around her own age. The one girl among them looked to Gem like she had gone out of her way to look as shocking as possible, and she frowned when she saw Gem. Of the three boys, the red-haired one with the freckles seemed even busier looking at the place than Gem had been, while the olive skinned one wearing torn jeans gave her a suspicious look that quickly turned to a smile. The third, who Gem had to admit was good-looking in a far too clean-cut, sure of himself sort of way, strolled over to her.

"Hi, I'm Stieg Sparks," he announced in a Texas accent. "Most people call me Sparks. You're here for the week?"

Gem nodded, then cocked her head to one side. She had heard the tiny note of surprise in that, and she knew the way jocks like this thought.

"What? Don't you think I should be?"

"No, it's just..."

"It's just that you don't look much like a gamer," the girl with the multi-hued hair said.

"And who are you?" Gem demanded.

"Katherine. Most people call me Kat."

She stuck out a hand like a challenge, and seemed surprised when Gem took it.

"Gemma," Gem replied.

'Everyone calls me Gem. You're British?"

"From London. North side of the river. I suppose someone's got to be." She paused, looking Gem up and down. 'So what are you doing here? Daddy buy you a way in?"

"Ignore Kat," the boy who had given her the suspicious look said. "It will be nice having someone so good-looking around. I'm Riordan Roberts. Rio."

Gem started to roll her eyes to Kat at that line, but the other girl's expression wasn't entirely friendly. Kat nodded to the remaining boy, who stood there looking like he couldn't make up his mind whether to say anything. "Since we're doing introductions, that's Jack, which is apparently short for Jackson."

Gem smiled at the red-haired boy.

"Hi. Where are you from, Jack?"

"A-Alaska. Did you know that this place was built some time in the twelfth century?" The second half of it came out in a rush, as if to make up for the nervous stutter at the start.

"Some time after 1141, following a charter of King Stephen, to be more exact," a voice said. "It's nice that you've done your research, Mr. Zusak."

Gem recognized the voice instantly as that of Henry Word. After his online announcements, she was hardly going to forget. He must have come into the hallway through a side door. She turned to greet him with the others, expecting to look up into the already half-familiar face, and had to adjust the direction of her gaze when it turned out that Henry Word was sitting down.

He was sitting down because he was in a wheel-chair.

It was quite a high tech wheelchair, obviously custom made and designed around Henry Word, but there was no escaping the fact that it was there. From the waist up, Mr. Word was dressed conser-vatively, even elegantly, in a suit and silk tie. From the waist down, his legs disappeared beneath a tartan blanket. They didn't appear again on the other side.

"A small accident from my army days," Henry word said, and Gem found herself wondering if he'd read her mind in the second it took to decide that the others probably looked just as surprised as she did. Gem realized that, in all the pictures she had seen of Henry Word either online or in magazines, not one had shown more than his head and shoulders.

Henry Word laughed then.

"I can see I've caught you all rather by surprise. Still, before I turn into the main topic of conversation, can I take a moment to welcome the five of you?' his gaze flicked to each of them in turn, and Gem guessed that he was matching names to faces in his mind. "You are all here, of course, because you have turned out to be some of the biggest fans of my little game. Congratulations on that. For the next week, you'll be staying in what I hope you'll find to be extremely comfortable surroundings, and you'll get the benefit of a very special surprise."

"What surprise?" Rio asked from behind Gem. Henry Word chuckled again.

"Ah, Riordan Roberts, I take it? Well, there is nothing to be suspicious about. In fact, I think that as fans, you will all enjoy this particular surprise. I have simply decided to allow you access to the tenth level of my game while we are here."

Gem felt her brow furrow.

"But Mr. Word, aren't there only nine levels?"

"That's true at the moment," Henry Word answered. "Anachronia is rather new. You will be among the first to play it. Still, let's not focus on that too much now, shall we? Chef has excelled himself in the Great Hall, and I'm sure you must all be hungry after your journeys."

He turned his wheelchair and headed back through the door he had come through, obviously expecting the five of them to follow. Gem hurried to keep up, even though what she really wanted was to demand more details from him. Well, most of her wanted to demand more details. Her stomach was happy to have dinner first. It had been a long flight.

The Great Hall was everything that the name promised. The ceiling towered upwards, and held a great brass and iron chandelier. Along with a few paintings, the walls held more shields and weapons, as though Henry Word expected an army to pop round for spares at some point, while the floors were wood that had been polished so much it reflected the light from above, making stepping on it like treading over a spray of stars.

There were two long tables, arranged with one down each side of the hall. Mr. Word showed the five of them to one table, then wheeled off towards the other, where half a dozen men and women dressed with varying degrees of formality.

"My advisors," he explained without being asked. "There is always so much to do. Still, at least this will give you all a chance to get to know one another."

Gem took the seat nearest to her, watching as the others arranged themselves around the table. Sparks glanced across to where Gem sat, then took the place next to Kat, while Rio wound up beside Jack.

"So Kat," Sparks asked, "what is it like living in London?"

Gem listened to Sparks and Kat talk for a while. She had been prepared for Kat to come off as odd, given how she dressed, but from what she could tell, the other girl was pretty normal. She also got the feeling that Kat would hate it if anyone pointed that out. Particularly if *Gem* pointed it out.

"So I was going to get this tattoo, once," Kat said at one point, "but my mum said no. She said I wasn't old enough. I..."

Gem switched her attention to the other conversation at the table. It was half a conversation, really. Jack seemed to be working hard to get Rio to talk. For his part though, Rio seemed to be ignoring the other boy as best he could.

"So whereabouts in LA are you from?"

"East."

"What's that like then? I bet it must be warmer than Alaska, right? Everywhere is warmer than Alaska."

"It's OK."

Somewhere in all of this, food arrived, carried by waiters who looked like they might have stepped out of a professional restaurant. The food was good, certainly better than anything served up at her school, and Gem kept listening to the others as she sipped at some soup she had to slow herself to keep from gulping down. She hadn't realized how hungry she was.

Kat and Sparks had got onto the subject of sport, where Kat had found out that the boy was a quarterback at his school. Gem could have told her that ten minutes ago. Some things were just obvious. Still, Kat seemed interested enough.

"Of course, over here, what we'd call football, you'd call soccer. Me, I'd rather just skate. You can take a board anywhere. Still it must be pretty cool."

Sparks said that it was, though to Gem, he didn't sound very convinced of it. Maybe Kat heard it too, quickly taking the conversation off into music. They didn't have many of the same tastes, but then, Gem suspected that not that many people would have managed to have exactly the same musical tastes as Kat. There were bands there that she'd never even heard of, and Kat seemed almost pleased when Sparks admitted that he hadn't heard of them either.

Between the two conversations, not to mention the arrival of yet more food, it wasn't easy to give much attention to what was happening on the other table. Still, Gem glanced across. Henry Word seemed to be discussing business with his advisors over dinner, and Gem wanted to see what he was like when he wasn't greeting visitors.

He seemed to be almost as friendly with his advisors as he had been with the five of them out in the lobby. He laughed and he joked, but Gem could still tell that he was very definitely in charge. The others deferred to him constantly, and he seemed to be very much the center of attention. Pleased to have found out that much about him, Gem turned her attention back to eating. Some of the other cheerleaders at school might have made fun of her for putting away so much, but they hadn't just spent hours on a plane, and this food was too good to miss in any case.

Besides, lurking behind it all was the thought that once they had finished dinner they might get to hear more about Anachronia, Henry Word's new Wordwick level. It was a thought that made Gem's fork practically fly over her plate.

SPARKS tried to keep up as Kat talked, but it wasn't easy. He found himself glancing hopefully at the other girl, Gem, but she just seemed happy to sit and watch the whole thing...

Rio watched her too. He wasn't sure what a little pretty rich girl like her was doing there, but he was certainly glad she was...

Jack was surprised that the other boy didn't have more to say. Hadn't he looked up the history of the castle before he came here? Jack kept going anyway, hardly noticing that Rio wasn't listening...

Kat kept talking, hoping to find a way through, before finally giving up. It wasn't like she cared. She was there to win a game, after all...

Through it, Henry Word watched them all. They were young, of course, but everything said that they should be perfect. Even so, he hoped that this would work...

Chapter 2

Eventually the dinner ended, and even Gem found herself full. Most of Henry Word's advisors drifted off when he announced that he was going to take the five winners on a tour of the castle. The only one who stayed was a balding man in slightly frayed tweed, whom Mr. Word introduced as Dr Percy Brown, his personal physician.

"Percy has been vital in keeping me running well enough to produce Wordwick, as well as making more than a few contributions himself. Hopefully he'll also make sure that I don't get you all hopelessly lost while I show you round."

"Lost? Hah!" Dr Brown stuck his hands in his pockets in a way that reminded Gem of one of her teachers. "You designed half of this place yourself.

It's the rest of us that have to worry about getting lost."

"Well then, another tour should help, shouldn't it?"

Gem and the others followed in the two men's wake as they started back towards the lobby. Gem found Sparks beside her as they walked.

"So what do you think of Henry Word?" he asked softly. Gem shrugged.

"He seems very confident," she whispered back. "But I guess he would be. His father was rich, and he's built up an empire of his own."

"You know a lot about him."

Gem wondered if she should mention that her father worked as his lawyer. Sparks seemed nice enough, but from the way he'd first greeted her, she suspected that he would think that had had something to do with her getting to be here. Kat had almost said as much.

"I just did some research."

If Sparks was going to say anything back, he was cut off as Henry Word drew to a halt.

"Right then, this is the lobby. From here, you can get to a few places that might interest you. If you would, Percy." He nodded to a door, and Dr

Brown opened it. Behind it stood a large, carpeted room filled from floor to ceiling with bookshelves. Instead of ladders to access the higher shelves, there were mechanical arms, similar to the ones found at fairgrounds to grab prizes, and connected to small screens with joysticks. Gem guessed that was probably easier for Mr. Word than having to call someone over every time he wanted a book. Probably more fun, too. A ring of great oak desks dominated the middle of the room, forming a circle around a marble bust of a man's head. Briefly, Gem thought it might be of Henry Word when he was younger, but there were enough subtle differences that she decided it had to be a relative.

"My father, William Ralph Word," Henry Word announced. "I thought I should have a statue of the old boy somewhere. There's a complete run of everything his newspaper empire put out too, though if you want something that won't put you to sleep, there's a lot of other stuff too."

He wheeled around and headed for one of the other doors. Gem got the feeling that Henry Word liked having everyone hurry to keep up. He threw open the next door, and they all scrambled through. It was a recreation room, Gem noticed, with a row of old-fashioned arcade machines along one wall, a pool table in the middle, and a few chairs off to one side surrounding a sleek looking music station. The chairs looked like the sort that more or less swallowed you up when you tried to sit down, so that you needed at least two attempts to get up.

"We usually keep the pool table set up for nine-ball," Henry Word said. "Don't play against Percy though. He's something of a pool shark."

"I am not!" Dr Brown complained. "I just happen to apply the basic principles of physics – "

"And he's easy to tease." Henry Word grinned as he said it. "Come on, let's take you to Percy's home-from-home. That should calm him down."

This door, Gem noted, had an electronic lock added to the wood. Henry Word punched in the combination and it swung open, revealing the sort of room that never should have lived behind a wooden door. A sliding, motion sensing, high-tech door perhaps, but not a wooden one.

The space was almost as big as the Great Hall, and wasn't cluttered up with things like long tables. All the tables here were individual workstations, holding computers, people working at the computers, and the sort of small fluffy toys that inevitably collect around them. The people were mostly casually dressed, and would occasionally look up to ask one another questions, but mostly they kept their eyes glued to the screens. The floor around the walls was a mess of wires, looking like someone had spilled a plate of spaghetti and then decided to connect it to the mains. Most of them ran into a blocky server station at one end of the room at some point.

"This is where we run Wordwick," Henry Word announced. "I've got some of the finest computer minds in the country, the world even, working constantly to build it, update it and keep it running."

"It's very impressive," Gem said. One of them had to.

"Impressive." Dr Brown shook his head. "Hardly. We're not running nearly as efficiently as we should be, and then there are the overheating problems, the-"

"I think that's our cue to leave Percy to it," Henry Word suggested, and the six of them left as the advisor started issuing instructions to people at the nearest terminals. "I think perhaps we should try the gardens next."

They did. Gem kept pace with the wheelchair, and Sparks kept up with her. Rio lagged behind a pace or two, as though showing enthusiasm about a garden wasn't the sort of thing you were supposed to do. Kat and Jack brought up the rear, mostly because Jack's own enthusiasm kept fixing on parts of the castle architecture, or particularly interesting heraldic shields, or any one of the hundred other things there were to catch a history buff's eye. As far as Gem could see, Kat was more or less dragging him along.

They followed Henry Word outside, then around the side of the main keep, through a small gate in a walled off area of the castle. Gem found herself hit by the scent of roses, and looked around to see them in every shade from white to the deepest red, growing on trellises, or out of flowerbeds, or around benches.

"This is beautiful," Gem said.

"You'd never be able to skate it properly though," Kat said from behind her. "And roses? It's so... girly. Just your sort of thing, probably," she added in Gem's direction.

"Well, everyone has their own opinion." Henry Word's tone was carefully diplomatic. "I kept the rose garden on from the previous owners. I find them rather peaceful."

That peace was briefly shattered as a screeching sound cut through the rose garden. Gem jumped at it. The only consolation was that it caught everyone else almost as much by surprise.

"What was that?" Rio demanded. "Some sort of cat?"

"It's a peacock," Gem guessed.

"That's right." Henry Word looked pleased. "You get used to the noise after a while, so don't let it bother you. If we are lucky, they will be out on the lawns where we can see them."

He led the way through the other side of the rose gardens, to a spot overlooking a garden that was more like a park in size. It had been laid out in ordered shapes that made it look like the pieces to some giant jigsaw puzzle from their vantage point.

"Another inheritance from the people I bought the place from," Henry Word explained. "Though they had let it go quite a bit. I learned that it had been laid out a few hundred years ago by the great garden designer Capability Brown, and I was able to find the plans. It seemed like a good idea to have it put back as it was."

He led them along the garden paths, and as Gem had noticed when she arrived, the gardens contained a maze of hedges that reached over head height. Given how uninterested she had been in the rose garden, Kat seemed to like the maze, asking how difficult it was to get through. She obviously caught Gem's surprised look at that, because she shrugged.

"What? I like puzzles."

The final stop on their tour was the castle's lake, which was really an extension of the moat. It stretched out for what had to be half a mile, and Gem could only just make out the small summerhouses and boathouses on the other side.

"This is even more space than back home," Sparks observed.

"Yeah, well imagine what it's like for the rest of us, farm boy," Rio muttered softly. Gem doubted that the other boy heard. Maybe Henry Word did though, because he chose that moment to bring the tour to a close, saying that they should get back to the house. He led the way again, and the two older boys kept pace. Gem found herself walking with Kat and Jack.

"So," she said to Jack, "what did you think of the tour?"

"It was... that is... I um..." he hurried away to catch the others.

"I think he must be nervous," Gem said to Kat.

"Funny that. He wasn't nervous around me."

They got back to the lobby ok, and Henry Word led them to the last of the doors leading off from it, which turned out to be for an elevator. He waited until they were all inside before speaking.

"Right, that's most of the tour. I will take you up to your rooms now, and you can settle in. You might want to get some sleep. Before that though, I know you have all been dying to find out more about Wordwick's Anachronia level, so I won't keep you waiting any longer.

"It's very straightforward really. Your goal when playing it will be to win the crown of the kingdom of Anachronia, using all your wits, skills and talents. The people will only give the crown to someone who can do three things: end the threat of the three-headed dragon terrorizing the land, unite the two warring clans that live there, and help the people of Anachronia flourish. Is that clear?"

Gem nodded. Several of the others did too.

"It sounds simple," Sparks said, beside her.

"Oh, it's not as easy as it sounds," Henry Word continued,

"which is why there are a few other things you should know. First, beware the Wickedly Woods where the dragon lives. It isn't the only danger there. Second, remember that you can work together, even if only one of you can rule in the end. Third, and most importantly, remember that words have power in Anachronia, finding the right words, the Ruler Words, along the way will make your time far easier."

The elevator came to a halt then, and Henry Word led them to a hallway that was almost a mirror of the lobby, except that the five doors here were open, and led to bedrooms. Gem could see that her bags had been brought up and left just inside the door to one of them. She walked over.

It was a surprisingly large bedroom, and it was warm thanks to the rows of tapestries covering the walls. There was a bookshelf with a few volumes, set above a small desk that stood next to a chest of drawers. The bed was a curtained four-poster affair that looked like it knew the same swallowing people up trick as the chairs in the recreation room.

The only thing that didn't fit lay on one side of the room, and it *really* didn't fit. It was as though the same people who had been so meticulous in finding genuine medieval objects to decorate the rest of the castle had suddenly thrown up their collective hands in defeat and shoved in something from a science fiction show. It was a pod, just a little larger than a person, made of a clear plastic substance with holes in it for air. There was a screen built into the open lid, along with a big red button that looked like the sort of thing they had on machinery to stop it in emergencies.

"Those are our gaming pods," Henry Word explained. "We think they will give you a... fuller gaming experience. Well, I'll let you all get to sleep. Goodnight."

As he left them, Gem knew that the others' eyes would be firmly on the pod in their room. She knew hers were.

JACK spent a couple of minutes looking at the pod before he climbed into it. It was even more interesting than the castle, and a lot easier to deal with than talking to beautiful girls. He lay down, checked briefly to make sure that his glasses were in place, and closed the lid...

Sparks took a little longer, mostly because he wanted to get a better look at how the thing worked. He was impressed. Whoever had designed this was a genius. With the sort of speed he normally reserved for dodging high-school linebackers, he leapt into the thing and let the top swing down...

Kat unpacked before she got round to the pod, though since her method of unpacking was simply to shove things into any drawer that looked about the right size, it didn't take long. When she did look at it, it occurred to her that it looked a bit like a coffin, so as she lay down she folded her arms and did her best to affect a Transylvanian accent, not entirely successfully. "Off to Anachronia ve go..."

Rio watched the pod for almost half an hour before he tried it. He was trying to think of all the angles this Word guy could be playing. Eventually though, he realized that the others had probably already begun using the pods. At the thought that the quarterback would probably already be there, showing off to the pretty blonde, he scrambled in and brought the lid down quickly. After all, the last thing he wanted was to look scared...

For her part, Gem had a couple of books open. One was a history of medieval Europe. Another was a dictionary. That was open to A, where she had penciled a ring around the word anachronism. Well, she thought, if there was ever a thing in the wrong historical period, it was the pod in the corner of the room. She took a deep breath, walked over, and lay down inside...

From Top Author for Young Adults
Kailin Gow

PULSE

17 year-old Kalina didn't know her boyfriend was a vampire until the night he died of a freak accident. She didn't know he came from a long line of vampires until the night she was visited by his half-brothers Jaegar and Stuart Greystone. There were a lot of secrets her boyfriend didn't tell her. Now she must discover them in order to keep alive. But having two half-brothers vampires around had just gotten interesting...

Want More Edgy books like *Bitter Frost*?

Enter

the EDGE

theedgebooks.com

Where you will find edgy books for teens and young adults that would make your heart pound, your skin crawl, and leave you wanting more...

Feed Your Reading Addiction

LaVergne, TN USA
27 August 2010
194889LV00004B/21/P